SPECIAL MESSAGE TO READERS

THE ULVERSCROFT FOUNDATION
(registered UK charity number 264873)

was established in 1972 to provide funds for research, diagnosis and treatment of eye diseases. Examples of major projects funded by the Ulverscroft Foundation are:-

- The Children's Eye Unit at Moorfields Eye Hospital, London
- The Ulverscroft Children's Eye Unit at Great Ormond Street Hospital for Sick Children
- Funding research into eye diseases and treatment at the Department of Ophthalmology, University of Leicester
- The Ulverscroft Vision Research Group, Institute of Child Health
- Twin operating theatres at the Western Ophthalmic Hospital, London
- The Chair of Ophthalmology at the Royal Australian College of Ophthalmologists

You can help further the work of the Foundation by making a donation or leaving a legacy. Every contribution is gratefully received. If you would like to help support the Foundation or require further information, please contact:

THE ULVERSCROFT FOUNDATION
The Green, Bradgate Road, Anstey
Leicester LE7 7FU, England
Tel: (0116) 236 4325

website: www.foundation.ulverscroft.com

SOMETHING'S BREWING

When Kate's job as a superstore manager comes to an abrupt end, she takes a risk and signs the lease to a seafront café. After hiring a teenage girl to work weekends, Kate is shocked to learn that her uncle is Ryan Scott, her former boss. He's tall, dark, attractive — and in Kate's opinion, arrogant. As she opens for business, she begins to see a different side to him. But with a café to run, Kate doesn't have time to think about Ryan, or any other man . . .

WENDY KREMER

SOMETHING'S BREWING

Complete and Unabridged

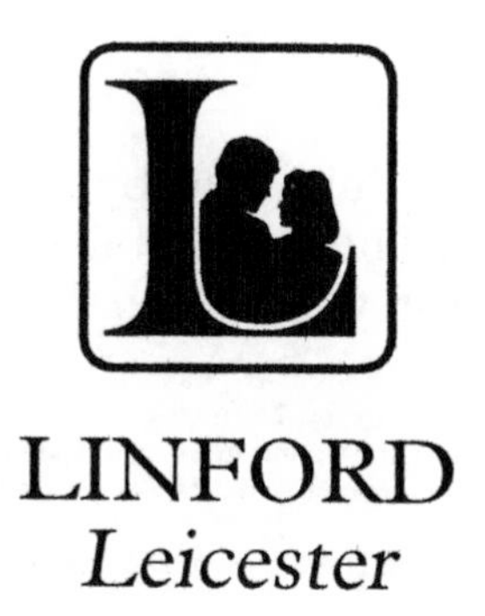

LINFORD
Leicester

First published in Great Britain in 2017

First Linford Edition
published 2019

A catalogue record for this book is available from the British Library.

ISBN 978–1–4448–4257–9

Published by
F. A. Thorpe (Publishing)
Anstey, Leicestershire

Set by Words & Graphics Ltd.
Anstey, Leicestershire
Printed and bound in Great Britain by
T. J. International Ltd., Padstow, Cornwall

This book is printed on acid-free paper

A Wise Decision?

Kate looked at the wall clock and pushed some loose strands of hair back under her scarf. Things were beginning to look good at last.

When she'd signed the lease for the café, many of her friends had declared she was mad. It was on the seafront, but it had been unoccupied for years.

The owner had grabbed her offer. She already knew he'd waited a long time for someone to show interest, because she'd asked various local people about it before she'd approached him. The shop's interior and general appearance had gone totally downhill. He'd offered Kate a reasonable fixed rent for the downstairs premises and the flat above the café for five years.

Since signing the contract, she'd persuaded and harassed plumbers and carpenters into action. The main work was finished, including the tiling of the customer and staff toilets.

Her brother Nick had promised to help this weekend with the painting. Next week the carpenters were installing the old wooden counter she'd bought from an old-fashioned, run-down grocery shop. A good wash with hot soda water would clean it and make it an eye-catcher. Its original state of unvarnished wood was just the effect she wanted.

Kate paused to drink lukewarm coffee from her flask. Thinking back over the last couple of weeks, she still couldn't quite believe it. She had been successfully managing a large superstore until the problem with Monica had changed everything.

Managing the store had never been Kate's dream job, but it had suited her qualifications, she did it well, and the salary was above average.

Monica had started the ball rolling. She worked mornings at the store and Kate often stopped to have a brief chat with her. She was a single parent with a little boy of four. Her husband had died unexpectedly and Kate admired how Monica was mastering her ill fortune.

Monica worked hard and was dependable. Until her husband's death, she'd headed the branch office of a national insurance company, and there was enough money to pay for her son's full-time care.

The new situation had forced her to give up her lucrative job to look after Tim. She took the part-time job at the supermarket to fill the gap, and hoped to find a better paid one that was more suited to her qualifications. Every time she applied, and they noted she was a single parent with a four-year-old son, they stated their misgivings and predictably she received a rejection.

One day, Kate's assistant, Susan, reported that someone had seen Monica stuffing a carton of 200 cigarettes into her bag. Kate was stunned. She prided herself on being good at judging character.

She called Monica into the office.

Monica guessed why, and tried to hide her anxiety.

'I'm sorry, Kate. It's a misunderstanding, but I realise that it doesn't look good. A neighbour asked me to bring him a carton of cigarettes. For a mad moment, I thought about pocketing the cigarettes and keeping the money towards my car instalments. I'm behind with payments.

'I need my car to take Tim to nursery and pick him up every afternoon. It's on the opposite side of the town. Tim loves it there and I don't want to move him until he's over his dad's death.

'As soon as I put the cigarettes into my bag, I knew I couldn't do it. I've never done anything dishonest before and I knew I wouldn't start now. Christina came along to collect me for the tea break just when I was about to put them back.

'I didn't want her to think badly of me, so I left them in my bag until after the break. Someone must have spotted me sticking the carton in my bag. I swear I did put them back at the very first opportunity.'

Kate shuffled the papers on her desk and looked up.

'It was utterly stupid of you. If you'd explained about your problem with the car instalments, I would have found another solution, like a temporary advance on your wages. Even if you have put them back, it was wrong of you to even consider doing it for a single second.'

Tears coursed down Monica's cheeks.

'I know. I'm so ashamed. I swear it's not how I normally act. I was a fool, but I did put them back. Since John died, I'm often disoriented and my thoughts and decisions run riot. My conscience told me straight away I was stupid. My parents would be terribly upset if they knew; they keep telling me they will help if I'm in a tight spot.'

Kate took a deep breath.

'I hope you realise I should fire you on the spot, but as the goods haven't actually left the premises, and I think you won't ever be as silly again, I'll ignore what's happened this morning and give you another chance.

'If anyone asks, make an excuse that you noticed the cigarettes were stacked amongst the wrong sort and then someone hurried you along for your tea break. You pushed them in your bag because you didn't want to forget to put them back among the right stack straight after the break.'

The shock and fear gave way to hopeful surprise on Monica's face and she nodded with her mouth slightly open. Rubbing the tears away with the back of her hand, she gulped.

'Thanks, Kate! I'll never forget it.'

'Get back to work and we'll have a word about your car problem another time. Perhaps you can get the dealer to change your present contract for a longer running time; that would lessen the pressure.

'Alternatively, perhaps he'll be prepared to exchange the one you have for a smaller, less expensive car, with lower repayments. I'm sure they'd rather have a customer who finishes paying than only getting half the payments back and the additional problem of selling a second-hand car.' Monica started to say something, but Kate brushed her words aside. 'You'd better get back to work before I change my mind.'

Monica scrambled to her feet and murmured thanks repeatedly as she scuttled out of the office.

Kate was lost in her thoughts about whether she'd done the right thing when Susan came in.

'How did she take it?' Susan asked. 'Do you want me to make sure that she empties her locker when she leaves?'

Kate busied herself with some papers.

'I didn't fire her. She realises it was terribly wrong and she put the cigarettes back straight away. She's had a hard time trying to cope since the death of her husband and I've decided to be lenient. She knows she won't get another chance.'

Susan's eyes flashed.

'You can't do that! You know it's

against company rules to condone theft. She was trying to steal. If you yield to every hard luck story, things here will soon spiral out of control.'

Kate couldn't argue with that and Susan knew it.

'Sometimes you have to decide what's best for everyone. She works hard and I'm sure she'll never even think about doing it again. She was desperate for money.'

'Huh! Aren't we all?' Susan pointed out. 'You're acting contrary to the rules.'

'I know, but it's my decision, not yours.' Kate lifted her chin. 'She stays.'

Susan didn't argue any further. Her eyes were stony with anger as she turned on her heel and went out, closing the door loudly behind her.

Handsome, but Arrogant

Kate wasn't too surprised when, a few days later, the inevitable happened. Susan had coveted Kate's job for a while and she'd played into her hands.

An anonymous report to headquarters had sparked a prompt reaction. The personnel department told her to fire Monica and notified her that the divisional manager would be calling soon to discuss her own future. Kate guessed what that meant.

She'd only met Ryan Scott at HQ meetings, or at area conferences. Her store ran well and there was no reason that she needed to justify herself on her visits to head office. Lots of stories circled about his management skills.

She'd heard that if a visitor to his office held long, unreasonable, and boring discourses, the next time he or she would find themselves standing, instead of sitting with coffee and biscuits. It speeded things up considerably. Kate judged him as a single-minded, ambitious, and very professional man.

She decided to hand in her notice before he turned up to haul her over the coals. Perhaps he'd want to crow over her misguided conduct before he finally dismissed her. He wouldn't get the chance.

Monica was very upset when Kate explained that powers beyond her control meant she had to fire her after all. Kate had already typed Monica a standard testimonial. She knew Monica would never get responsible work again if a hint of wrongdoing appeared on her reference. Monica didn't even read it. She took it, nodded, and left without another word.

Susan pretended to sympathise, but Kate knew she could barely hide her glee. As she'd undoubtedly been the one who had informed headquarters about what had happened, Kate had difficulty in not accusing her outright of being hypocritical and disloyal.

The sales people in the store were supportive. The news about what had happened spread like wildfire. Everyone knew that Kate was leaving because her compassion and kindheartedness had led to her downfall.

Kate was still entitled to some holidays, so she decided to clear her desk, and get out fast. On her final day, as a gesture of solidarity, a representative from the working staff gave her a bouquet of flowers. She felt emotional to see her staff were still loyal and supportive.

Packing her personal things into a cardboard box, she put the beautiful bouquet of tulips on top and prepared to leave. She straightened the items on her desk and glanced around for the last time.

When the sound of the door opening interrupted the silence, she looked up and had to draw a deep breath.

'Good morning!' Ryan Scott considered the cardboard box in her arms. 'I see I'm almost too late.'

She found her voice again.

'Good morning, Mr Scott. Yes, I was just on my way out.' She indicated the desk.

'I've left everything up to date. If you have any questions, I'm sure Susan will help.' Kate had seen him fairly often at meetings, but never this close up. He was much taller than she remembered and much more attractive.

His dark brows straightened and he regarded her carefully.

'We need to talk. Your resignation arrived at headquarters two weeks ago. I was in London at the time on a management course, and didn't find out about the situation until I got back yesterday.'

Kate shrugged and clenched her teeth tighter.

'It doesn't make any difference. I acted contrary to company rules.' She met his glance without flinching. 'In case you want to know why, I don't think it's wrong for managers to be tolerant sometimes. The woman concerned was a good worker. She put the cigarettes back straight away because she knew it was wrong. I also knew that if she lost her job her life would be even more difficult for her than it is already.'

With a shadow of annoyance on his face as he brushed her words aside, his dark brown eyes remained puzzled.

'Yes, I've read all about the whys and wherefores.' He hesitated before he went on. 'Rules are rules. However, I've spoken with some of the workers downstairs and they are all on your side. They assured me you acted with the very best of intentions. Usually most workers complain constantly — yours have hardly ever grumbled — today or on any other occasion.'

He shifted his weight.

'I'm prepared to overlook what's happened. You have a very good record and this is the first time anything of this kind has cropped up.' He took her envelope out of his pocket and put it down on the desk. 'Your resignation

. . . We'll just forget what's happened, shall we?'

It maddened Kate that he looked so smug and condescending, as if he were offering her a personal gift.

She also admitted that, although she'd barely spoken with him for more than a few minutes previously, something about him had always impressed her, and right now she definitely didn't want to be interested in any man.

He irritated her, and not just because of his good looks or because he was well groomed, but also because he clearly knew what he wanted and how to get it.

Admittedly, other colleagues who knew him better conceded that he worked harder than anyone else did at his level of management, and that he deserved his success. There was no logical reason why she should dislike him.

She considered him closely for a moment. His business suit, pristine white shirt and conservative tie were from no second-class source. Kate still didn't understand why she felt edgy in his presence.

She wasn't doubtful about her abilities and she knew she was good at her job. He'd never had a reason to criticise her.

Her thoughts returned to the present. She picked up the envelope and handed it back to him.

'Thank you, but I've already made other plans.'

* * *

Ryan shrugged without any further comment and slipped the envelope into his pocket.

Still puzzled by her refusal, he watched as Kate marched towards the door and tried to open it whilst juggling the box in her arms. Before he moved to offer help, she'd exited, and closed the door by hooking her foot around it and pulling.

He thought about the envelope in his

breast pocket and wondered who to appoint as her successor.

Her assistant wasn't suitable, he decided. She'd soft-soaped him when he'd arrived just now; that was never a good sign.

He deduced she was probably the whistle blower. He also didn't like the fact that she hadn't supported her boss. It made no difference if Miss Watson had been right or wrong, anyone who was lower in rank should always be supportive, and clever enough to present the right kind of arguments to change their boss's mind if necessary.

It was a pity. Kate Watson was good at her job. There had been few complaints or problems from this store. He recalled that she'd never been pushy at meetings, although she expressed her opinion with resolve whenever asked.

He liked her arresting oval face, with its defined cheekbones, smooth skin, and generous mouth. He also liked the way she dressed; classical with muted colours. An easy smile played at the corner of her mouth when she talked to someone she knew and liked. Ryan was surprised how much he'd remembered even though they'd rarely spoken.

He checked his watch. Time to get back to headquarters and check through the possible candidates. He had to fill the gap as soon as possible.

Early Days

A couple of weeks later, Kate looked through the dirty windows at the esplanade and beyond that to the wall several feet above the beach.

Today the sea was dark and sombre, and the waves angry as they charged inland to dissolve on to the sand.

The time of year wasn't encouraging for a budding café owner, but she also knew that soon she'd see delightful shafts of light patterned on peaceful water, sunshine streaming down, and people wandering the beach in their bare feet.

Her notice in the window 'Tearoom Opening Soon' already made people peer inside to see what was going on. That was a good sign.

Her mobile phone rang.

It was Monica Wells. Her voice was cautious.

'Hello, Kate! I heard you lost your job because of what happened. I want you to know how sorry I am. I hope you have time to come around for coffee.'

Kate didn't feel any resentment.

'Don't worry. I left of my own free will. It's kind of you to invite me, but I'm in the middle of painting. The carpenters will be back on Monday and I have to finish the painting by then.'

'I heard about your tearoom. One of the other girls from the supermarket told me all about it. How courageous and exciting! What time do you finish?'

'I keep going until the light fades. You can't see the missed spots in artificial light.'

'I'd offer to help you with the painting, but bringing Tim makes things awkward. Why don't you come here today after you finish. That's if you've nothing else planned, of course. Timmy will be in bed by then. I'll make us something to eat.'

'I smell of paint, and I'm probably

plastered in the stuff, too.'

Monica laughed lightly.

'I don't mind. I feel terribly guilty about what happened. I tried to contact you as soon as I heard. Susan wouldn't give me your telephone number. Babs on the switchboard had it and gave it to me without quibbling.'

Kate laughed softly.

'Typical of Babs. She had it for emergencies. Don't feel guilty; in fact, I'm grateful to you. I might never have tried something else if it hadn't happened.'

'Do you have any plans for this evening, then?' Monica persisted.

'No, not really. Just a bath and an early night.'

'Then please come and have a meal with me. I promise I won't keep you if you then feel tired and want to go home.'

Kate chuckled. The concept of someone making her something decent to eat was tempting. She lived on sandwiches or fell into bed without bothering. The waistband on her trousers was already very slack.

'OK, give me your address. Is some time after six all right with you?'

* * *

A few hours later, Kate drove down a tree-lined avenue to an end bungalow with neat flower-beds and a child's tricycle in the middle of the front lawn. Monica threw the door open as she was climbing the entrance steps.

'I saw you arriving. Come in! I'm so glad you could make it.' There was a delicious smell in the air and Kate realised she was hungry. 'Straight ahead. The living-room faces the back, towards the main garden.'

Kate went down a light passageway into a room with modern furnishings in tasteful colours. There was a small dining area in one corner and the table was set for two.

'I expect that you're hungry if you've been working all day. I've made us soup for starters, some asparagus wrapped in ham, and a chocolate gateau for dessert.'

'Sounds wonderful! Is Tim in bed? I was hoping to meet him.'

'Another time perhaps. He's on the move all day and by six o'clock he's tired out. Would you like to freshen up while I heat the soup? It's the first door on the right next to the front door.'

'Oh, yes, please! I feel so tatty.'

Kate felt much better for a quick wash. She brushed her hair and mused that she hadn't bothered about make-up for several days. Her skin also felt dry and neglected as she looked at her pale face in the mirror.

The meal was delicious. They chatted quite easily. The garage owner who'd sold Monica's husband their car was understanding about the repayments and Monica found he was looking for someone to cope with his paperwork. He was happy to employ her and she could work from home, unless he needed her for a special reason.

'He has grandchildren himself, and is very understanding. It doesn't pay a lot, but enough to support us, and I don't need to depend on benefits.'

'What about the bungalow? What about mortgage payments?'

'I used Colin's life insurance to pay off the remaining mortgage and there was enough left to establish a small trust for Timmy. The rates, electricity and so on still make a big hole in my income, but somehow we're managing. My parents want to help, but I don't want to involve them unless it's absolutely necessary. They deserve to enjoy their old age. I know they're always there if things get really desperate.'

Her eyes twinkled and Kate was glad to see that Monica looked more cheerful.

'What about you?' Monica asked. 'I know you're opening a teashop. How are you getting on?'

Kate told her how she'd always wanted to own a teashop and how she'd searched for the right premises. She described the work she'd done and what still had to be done. Leaning back, she smiled.

'I'm enjoying it immensely. I just hope I've chosen the right spot. The holiday season starts soon and I have to be ready by then.'

Monica handed her a plate with a large piece of chocolate gateau.

'Gosh, that looks gorgeous,' Kate told her. 'The whole meal was delicious, thank you. This cake reminds me that I still need someone to supply me with home-made cakes. Where did you get this one?' She tried a forkful. 'Mmm! Heavenly. Just right. Rich in chocolate and not too sweet. It melts in the mouth.'

'I'm glad you like it.' Monica poured them some coffee. 'I didn't buy it. I made it. I've always loved cooking and baking. I went to a couple of courses on cake decoration, and I have a shelf full of recipe books in the kitchen. John loved cake, and I could experiment.'

She sounded wistful as she stared

ahead, then turned to Kate and smiled again.

'Timmy isn't old enough to notice what kind of cake he's eating, so I'm not motivated to experiment much any more. I really enjoyed making this one after our telephone call this afternoon.'

Kate's brows lifted.

'It tastes wonderful and looks really professional.' Kate had a sudden thought. 'Would you consider making cakes for me? Do you have enough time? I can't even tell you how many I'll need, or how often yet. I was hoping to find someone who makes home-made cakes and who is flexible, because the demand might fluctuate.'

'Me?' Monica's voice squeaked slightly. 'Do you mean it?'

'If your other cakes are as good as this and you can offer a variety, I'm sure they'll pull in the customers. We could work out a system of payment based on ingredients plus cooking time, plus a fixed payment per cake. You'll need to think seriously about whether you'd like to do it. It would tie you down.'

Monica's cheeks were pink.

'Oh, I'd love to. I could make the cakes in addition to my job with the garage. I don't just do very rich or decorative cakes like this one, Kate. I enjoy making traditional things like sponges, or Madeira cake.'

'Sounds perfect.' Kate took another forkful of the cake and it melted on her tongue. 'I wish I'd brought a bottle of wine with me, then we could have toasted our future business relationship.'

Monica stood up.

'I have some wine I've been saving for a special day. This is one. I'll get it!'

Kate made a mental note that she would repay Monica's hospitality in some way as soon as she could.

Help Is at Hand

Ten days later Kate was exhausted but satisfied.

She'd wanted the café to be elegant in a minimalist sort of way, and for it to fit in with the world of the beach and the seaside town.

The wooden counter was in place and it had been a challenge for the carpenter and his helpers to get it into the right position in one piece.

It now dominated the end of the room, in front of the shelves already stocked with plain white crockery and other tableware.

Kate had been delighted when she discovered there was a beautiful slate floor under the cracked linoleum, even though she realised it would be too cold in autumn or winter. She would then cover the area under the tables with round red-edged sisal mats.

The wooden chairs matched the counter. They were unpretentious in style with clean straight lines and high backs. She'd found a local shop who'd made loose red cushions for the backs, and thicker, more comfortable ones, for the seats.

Her carpenter had found a number of small round tables in a wholesaler's, and he'd sanded and varnished the surfaces to match the counter as closely as he could.

He had also positioned one long antique refectory table with a backless bench against an inside wall and Kate positioned chairs on its opposite side for larger groups who wanted to sit together.

She'd painted the walls in a cheerful mixture of apricot and amber. Light flooded the room from the tall mullioned windows looking out on to the esplanade. It looked a friendly and inviting place to stop for coffee and cakes.

A bunch of noisy schoolchildren caught her attention when Kate was still busy with last-minute cleaning. The girls wore pleated maroon box skirts reaching down to their knees, long-sleeved white blouses, high socks, and dark pumps. Some of their blouses were hanging messily over their skirts.

The boys wore grey trousers, long-sleeved white shirts and maroon jackets. The boys and girls both wore ties criss-crossed in two colours. They walked in pairs, jostling and crowding each other as they competed for attention.

A couple of them were smoking. One girl was a few steps behind the others and seemed to be dragging her feet. The boy at the front decided to demonstrate his leadership skills. He had a stick in his hands and ran it across advertising boards outside the neighbouring shop, knocking one over. Encouraged by the ensuing laughter, he moved as if to run it across Kate's windows.

She dashed out.

'Hey! Leave off, you lot! Go and make a noise elsewhere.'

One of the other boys sniggered.

'What's the matter, love? Can't stand a bit of noise?'

'I don't want to have to clean my windows again just because you want a bit of fun. If you mess up my windows, I'll visit your headmaster, get your name and address, and have a word with your parents.'

'My old man wouldn't care,' the leader sneered.

'Wouldn't he? Even when he gets a letter instructing you to attend court for causing a public nuisance?'

The quiet girl at the back spoke up.

'Lay off, Roger. Let it be. It's not worth arguing about.'

'Why don't you just shut up, Kim?' One of the other girls, with bleached hair and bright red nails, answered spitefully.

'You're lucky we let you come with us. Don't try our patience.'

The others stood around looking awkward, but their leader noticed the people from the next-door shop were coming out and he began to saunter on, looking unconcerned while deliberating how to highlight his leadership once more before they headed back to school. The others began to follow in a straggling line.

The girl called Kim turned to head off in the other direction. Kate felt guilty as it looked like she had caused a rift between Kim and the others.

'Hey,' Kate called to the girl. 'Thanks for your support. How about a cola?'

The girl hesitated, then nodded.

Kate exchanged a few words with her neighbours and went inside to get the drink from the stock room. Standing by the counter, the girl looked round with interest. Kate handed her the opened bottle.

Kim took it.

'Thanks.' She took a gulp. 'There isn't another teashop in the town, is there? You'll do a good trade, I expect.'

'I hope so. I don't want to cause trouble between you and your friends . . . '

She shook her head, but looked troubled.

'They're not my friends. Not really.' She paused. 'I only moved here a couple of weeks ago and making new friends isn't easy.'

'Yes, I know. The same thing happened to me when my mum and dad moved house. It took me a while to adjust, but I think it also taught me to be more independent. I learned how important it is to follow your own instincts about people. I remember very well when some of them began to be friendly and were prepared to give me a chance even though I was a new face. Some of the others never wanted to bother.'

The girl nodded and her blonde ponytail bobbed briskly.

'It's not easy, though. The schoolwork's OK, but breaks and lunchtime are my main problem. I don't want to stand around like a lollipop lady, so I try to be friendly, but most of them have their fixed gangs and buddies; they're not looking for any additions.'

Kate nodded.

'I know how you feel. It was hard at first. I used to bury my nose in a book until the bell rang. The teachers on duty were good at stopping any bullying. What are yours like?'

'They're OK.' Kim shrugged.

'Well, don't put up with any bullying. Tell them to back off. Tell them to leave you alone. If they don't, you can threaten to report them, and get people at home involved. In my case, it took a couple of weeks until some of them decided I was OK. From then on it got a lot better.'

Kim looked thoughtful.

'The idea with reading a book is worth a try, I suppose. I'm not hiding and not getting in anyone's way either.' She took another sip.

'They won't change their attitude overnight, but I think you have enough self-confidence to challenge any direct bullying, and the decent ones will give you a chance after a while, I'm sure. Do you live in the town?'

Kim shook her head.

'Not around here. We're on the edge of things in one of the bungalows on the cliff top. I'm staying with family. My parents are in Sierra Leone for six months. I wanted to go with them, but they said that it wasn't a good idea.'

'What are they doing there?'

'My father is director of some boring company or other. He'll be there for at least another six, perhaps even nine months. My mother decided Dad needed her company more than I did.'

Kate laughed.

'I bet it wasn't that easy for them. I bet they considered the pros and cons of having you with them, or not, very carefully. Perhaps there are no suitable schools, and it would mean you'd lose a whole year of schooling. You're living with relatives until they return?'

'Yeah, with my uncle — my mum's brother. He's lived here for a couple of years.'

'Well, try to make the best of it. How old are you?'

'I'll be seventeen soon.'

Kate had an idea.

'If you haven't made friends yet, and

are bored at the weekends, would you like to work for me for a couple of hours on a Saturday and Sunday? I can't afford full-time help until I know the café is a success, but I need help at the weekends. That's when I'm expecting the most customers.'

Kim's expression lightened.

'That sounds great! The weekends are boring and I'm fed up with my uncle thinking up special outings just because he knows I'm bored.'

'Make sure he doesn't mind. Tell him I can give you a lift home after we close. If he doesn't object, let me know. I'm planning to open next weekend.'

'Brilliant! I'm sure he won't mind. He'll be glad to get rid of me for a couple of hours.' She looked at her watch. 'I have to get back to school. We shouldn't leave the school grounds during the lunch hour, but I was so fed up that when they asked me I tagged along. I'm glad I did now, otherwise I would never have met you, Miss . . . ?'

'Watson, Kate Watson, but you can

call me Kate. And you are?'

'Kim. Kim Chalmers.'

With a grin on her face, her blue eyes sparkling, and her ponytail bobbing back and forth, Kim set off at a run in the direction of the school.

Taste of Things to Come

Kate's brother turned up unexpectedly the next day. He'd helped with the painting and he nodded his approval when he looked around at the result.

'It looks good. It's in the right location and you're all ready to go.' He threw his arm around her shoulder. 'I remember you playing with doll's tea sets and you used to talk about owning a teashop even when you were at grammar school. I thought it was a pipedream, especially after you went to uni.'

Kate smiled.

'Because I thought I ought to be sensible and believed I'd be satisfied with a nine to five job and financial security. I'm so glad I've decided to give myself this chance.'

'What about the financial side of things?'

'That's where my business training helps. I have no real experience about catering, but I know what you need to offer — quality and customer service. You also need enough working capital to survive for at least a year.

'I'm going to offer cross-seasonal items like gift baskets, chocolates, and even local delivery. I've pumped my savings into the renovations. I'm selling my flat and I've decided to move into the flat on top of the shop, instead of sub-letting it. I'm fairly sure the bank will give me credit in an emergency so I can keep the flat's selling price in my savings account.

'I won't take any unnecessary risks. In effect, all I'm doing so far is investing in my future. Let's have a coffee!'

Kate had barely put the crockery on the table when the door opened and Monica came in. She had a cake container in one hand and a little boy in the other. Tim was pointing outside.

'Look, Mummy!'

Monica tried to appease him.

'We'll go to the beach after I've given Kate some cake, I promise.'

Tim frowned but he protested no further. Monica looked around.

'It looks fabulous.' She noticed Nick. 'Oh, sorry, I won't interrupt. I came to bring you another trial cake.' She offered the container.

Kate took it and laughed softly.

'Come in. Meet my brother. This is Nick.' She gestured towards Nick. 'Nick, this is Monica and Tim. Monica is my find of the century. She's a genius with a whisk and a wooden spoon.'

The two of them acknowledged each other and smiled.

'What is it this time?' Kate asked, looking at the container.

'Coffee cake, with Irish cream icing!'

'It sounds wonderful. We were just going to have some coffee, so you've come at a perfect moment. Sit down. There is a child's chair over there in the corner.'

Nick went to fetch it and they were soon seated and munching happily on some mouth-watering slices of cake.

Tim soon left them to wind his way through the chairs, playing trains.

'What do you do, Nick?' Monica asked.

'I'm a teacher. Maths and physics.'

She pulled a wry face.

'I was rotten at both.'

Nick laughed.

'I know they're not the most popular subjects, but perhaps that's why I like teaching them. Most children don't like them either at first. I try to make them likeable.'

'This cake is wonderful,' Kate proclaimed. 'What do you think, Nick?'

He took another forkful.

'Fantastic! Extremely good.' He eyed Monica. 'I don't get any home-made cake unless I visit my mother. Kate can bake, but it doesn't compare with this. This is brilliant!'

Nick noticed Tim had his nose pressed up against the window.

'I think a walk would do us all good, don't you? The weather's not bad for this time of year.'

They looked out and saw that grey clouds edged in white were making room for timid beams of sunshine and they nodded agreement.

A few minutes later, the cool onshore breeze blew at them as they descended the steps on to the sand. The sea waves carried a salty smell that made Kate conjure up fishing fleets and fishing nets swaying in the breeze, waiting for repairs.

They all took off their shoes because Tim wanted to run barefoot. The sand was cool, firm and smooth beneath their feet and the wind tangled and tousled their hair.

Kate looked at Monica and saw how relaxed she looked. The fact that she now had a little more security was working wonders.

Tim went down to the edge of the sea with Nick and shrieked with laughter as the water came, kissed his toes, and slipped away again.

Kate and Monica stood watching

them as the salt air ripped at their hair and faces.

'I'm so glad I came this afternoon. It's wonderful to see Tim enjoying himself.'

Kate nodded.

'Your husband's death must have been an awful shock for both of you.'

Her eyes misted.

'Yes, it was, but at least I understood what had happened. I don't think Tim has yet. I try to make sure he doesn't think that it had something to do with him or me, but you can only guess what goes on inside a child's mind.' She watched the two figures down by the water's edge. 'He seems to like your brother. That doesn't happen very often. Tim is shy with strangers.'

'Perhaps it's because Nick is used to children. His pupils are a lot older than Tim, but I presume that good teachers have an aura of understanding about them.'

Monica rubbed her hands together, nodded, and stuck them in her pockets.

'So your tearoom is nearly ready. Does it have a name yet?' she asked Kate.

'Something's Brewing.'

Monica laughed.

'I saw another café called that somewhere else and liked it,' Kate explained. 'Did I tell you I've found a girl to help me out on Saturdays and Sundays? She seems a nice kid and she's very enthusiastic. I hope that you'll come on opening day, too. What cakes do you suggest?'

'What about a Black Forest tart, a batch of lemon tartlets, some profiteroles you can fill according to needs with fresh whipped cream, and an iced carrot cake? You mentioned you intend to offer afternoon teas, so that means scones as well. Scones are easy to make. If you run out, just phone and I'll bring them over.'

Kate smiled.

'That sounds perfect. I wonder what the response will be. Perhaps I'll stand behind the counter all weekend, waiting for customers who never come.'

Monica shook her head vigorously.

'It's going to be a huge success. I can feel it in my bones.'

No Settling for Second Best

Kate hadn't slept very well. She was nervous and got up early. When she reached the teashop, the morning mist over the sea was just lifting. Occasional wisps of sunshine were fighting their way through the clouds to pattern the tips of the pewter-coloured sea with splashes of white and gold. The esplanade was empty.

Something special was about to happen in her life and her spirits lifted as she unlocked the door and went inside.

The fresh salty air invaded the room and lifted her spirits. Wrapping then tying the white apron over her black jeans, she straightened her blouse and carried the board outside that announced this was the place to stop for coffee and cake.

She positioned it between her shop and the one next door selling souvenirs and postcards. She didn't know the couple running the shop very well yet, but they'd exchanged greetings several times and the man had wished her luck yesterday.

She didn't expect customers for a while, so she fiddled with the crockery, then the single red tulip and green leaf in the plain white vases on the tables, and checked the cutlery for any sign of smudges. She surveyed the cakes waiting in the display case and started the coffee machine.

Taking a mug of coffee, she went to stand in the doorway and looked towards the sea. She'd done the right thing; she had seldom felt so right and happy with her life.

A short time later, the fresh bread arrived from a local baker. Monica brought her cakes and a supply of fresh scones and Tim tagged along beside her.

The local florist delivered a 'Good Luck!' green leafy plant from Kate's parents. It fitted nicely in one of the awkward corners and softened the minimalistic look. It was a perfect final addition.

Monica didn't stay long. She looked around approvingly, holding Tim by the hand.

'It's perfect, Kate. All your hard work has been worthwhile. I have to go. My parents are coming for breakfast and are staying for the rest of the day. If you need anything — scones or cake, or anything else — let me know and I'll bring it. I'm only ten minutes away in the car.' She hugged Kate. 'Good luck, and stop worrying. It's going to be a roaring success!'

Kate nodded.

'Thanks. If I can entice customers in, I'm sure your cakes will bring them back.'

Monica patted her arm.

'They'll come, and when they see this place, they'll continue to come back, I'm sure.'

The people from the shop next door arrived with a bunch of flowers.

Lottie was a redhead with glasses and twinkling blue eyes, and Ken was fresh faced and welcoming.

'All the best, love,' he declared. 'The town needed a place like this. I think you'll do well. If there's any trouble, you know where to find us.'

Kim was on time, and their first customers were sitting at one of the window tables a couple of minutes after they opened.

There was soon a steady stream of comings and goings. Both of them were new to waiting at tables, but if customers noticed, they didn't comment. Most people chose sandwiches with their tea or coffee at this time of the day, so Kate was busy behind the counter making small triangles of sandwiches with various contents, and making pots of coffee or tea.

As lunchtime approached, some people asked if they had a lunchtime menu, but had to be content with toasted sandwiches. Kate wondered if it would pay to have one or two home-made soups on offer. She made a mental note to talk to Monica about the possibility.

Nick arrived about midday and looked around with approval. Leaning over the counter he gave her a peck on her cheek.

'It looks like you've made it.'

'Some of them are just curious. The test will come when they know what it's like and still come back.'

'Don't be so pessimistic. Everyone looks very satisfied. A lot of your customers will be day visitors, but I expect local people will come, too, when they know there's a café in the neighbourhood.

'Have you put an advert in the local paper yet to remind people about reserving tables? That shows you're in demand and tables might not always be free.'

Kate laughed softly.

'Advice taken!' She looked at the display case on the counter with the remaining scones. 'I didn't think the scones would go so fast. There aren't enough for afternoon teas. I just phoned Monica and asked her to make a couple more batches. I don't like bothering her today because she told me her parents were visiting, but I have no choice. Would you be a love and pick them up for me? It would save her a journey.'

Nick tilted his head and grinned.

'Of course, no problem. I'm here to help a budding entrepreneur in any way I can. Where does she live? Phone and tell her I'm on my way.'

The whole day went well. Kim was enthusiastic and a great help. As time went on Kim declared that from now on she would always feel great sympathy for waiters.

Nick returned with the scones and mentioned that he'd met Monica's parents and that Tim was delighted to see him.

'I had to promise to build sandcastles with him on the beach when the weather allows. He's a nice kid.'

'Perhaps he's unconsciously looking

for a replacement father.' Kate studied him more carefully. 'How do you feel about that? Are you interested in Monica?'

'Good heavens — why do women take giant steps all the time? I've only just met her! I'm not sure about anything in that direction yet, and don't be so nosy.'

'But you like her?'

'Of course, she's a nice person, but . . . '

'You're hesitant because of Tim.'

'I haven't even thought of asking her out yet. It would be a big step for anyone, man or woman, to take on a ready-made family. It was straightforward with Johanna. I thought she loved me and I loved her, but look what happened.'

'Johanna was a career girl and she didn't intend anything to get in the way of her plans for the future. You messed that up and she was forced into choosing.'

'Yes, you're probably right.' His eyes twinkled. 'We could write the agony column in the newspaper between us, couldn't we?'

'I'm glad Simon moved on, he wasn't the earth-shattering experience I thought love would be. I sometimes wonder if love is an illusion. I'm not talking about the brainless short-lived kind that film stars and pop stars have all the time, I'm talking about love between people like Mum and Dad, who have been together for over thirty years and are still going strong. The excitement might have fizzled out, but love, respect, and perfect understanding have remained.'

He shrugged and she ruffled his hair.

'If I don't find 'The One' I'll still be fine,' Kate said. 'I'm not worried. Are you?'

'No, I've got a good life and I'm enjoying it,' he said. 'If I meet somebody I like it'll be great, if not . . . that's OK, too. I've learned that second best doesn't work. There's no point in pretending.

'By the way, Duncan says he wishes you luck, and he might pop in tomorrow,' Nick added. 'I think he'd prefer to be a permanent feature, but you're not interested, are you?'

She shook her head.

'Duncan is a love and a nice guy. I like him. Even if he is your best friend, I'm definitely not looking for a relationship with him, or anyone else.'

'You shouldn't let Simon colour your attitude for ever more.'

'I don't and I won't. It's just like you and Johanna. Simon was a mistake. I'm glad I found out in time. I now realise we were very different characters. He was into partying, knowing the right people, wearing the right clothes, and knowing which wine went with which meat. He grasped we didn't gel long before I did.

'It didn't really hurt when he rode off into the sunset with Sophia on his arm. He wasn't the love of my life. Sophia's greatest challenge is deciding to wear Banyan or Cardin sunglasses when the sun comes out. They suit each other perfectly. He'd have a heart attack if he saw me working in a café.'

Nick frowned.

'I never liked him. The man is an idiot. He's a human display doll with the brains of an ostrich.'

Kate chuckled.

'Don't insult ostriches!'

Shock from the Past

As the afternoon progressed, Kate put Nick in charge of the coffee machine, so that she could concentrate on preparing people's orders. She was pleased by the number of people who chose the afternoon tea — a tiered cake stand with small sandwiches at the bottom, scones with cream and jam in the middle, and cake on top. It was four o'clock by the time things started to slow down.

The doorbell pinged as Kate was preparing an order at the counter. She looked up and her mouth fell open. When Ryan Scott saw her, he looked just as flabbergasted, but only for a fleeting moment. He hesitated before he walked towards her.

Kim cut in on his progress and came with him to the counter.

'Kate, this is my Uncle Ryan,' she

announced. 'He promised to come, and he did.'

Kate met his brown eyes and was lost for words. He was someone she never expected to see again. She thought she'd escaped her past life completely. Her throat was as dry as sandpaper, but she managed a hesitant nod.

'Hello,' she mumbled.

Kim and Nick looked at them both, and noted the strained expressions.

'It looks like you already know each other,' Nick remarked.

Ryan recovered quickest.

'Yes, we do. We once worked for the same company.' He gave Nick his attention as if Kate were a mere bystander. 'I didn't know Miss Watson was the owner of this café.'

Kate guessed he didn't intend to enlighten Nick any more about the company.

'We didn't have a lot to do with each other in work,' she said quickly, seeing Nick's growing curiosity.

Ryan's eyes narrowed slightly and he paused.

'I tried to persuade Kim that she didn't need to work here at weekends, but she was quite determined.'

'Well, I'm glad that Kim agreed to help,' Kate said. 'She's been great. Never a grumble.'

'I hope not. You shouldn't complain about what you choose to do of your own free will.' He looked around. It was hard to tell if he approved of what he saw or not. 'She told me you close at six. I came to see where she was working, and also to take her home.'

Kim looked up at a couple of people just arriving.

'Another half an hour should do it, Ryan.' Kim smirked. 'Have a coffee and a piece of cake. The cassis cheese is mouth-watering and cheesecake is your favourite.'

'I came to take you home.'

Kate believed he was just being awkward.

'It's OK, Kim. I can manage. Off you go.'

Looking uncomfortable, Ryan's expression faltered.

'How did it go?' he asked Kim, evidently deciding to be more sociable.

'It was fine,' Kim answered then turned to Kate. 'I'll see you at the same time tomorrow.'

Kate smiled at her and ignored her uncle.

Not understanding why this woman with her resolute, unyielding expression bothered him so much, and why she'd made him sound tight-lipped when there was no logical reason, he tried to sound more forthcoming.

'Well, it's up to you. I hope you've done your homework,' he added.

Kim looked exasperated.

'Ryan, I did all my homework last night. I'm not stupid.'

He relaxed and automatically smiled at Kim.

Kim wasn't the only one who saw his smile and reacted positively. Kate's opinion softened for a moment. Why wasn't he more accommodating generally? Kim was acting positively for a girl of her age. She wasn't hanging around street corners, mixing with the wrong kind of friends, and she wasn't afraid of work, either.

He grinned at his niece and gestured with his thumb.

'OK, then. Get your coat, Kim. I'm parked round the corner.'

Kim went off, leaving the two of them eyeing each other.

'There is no need for you to come for Kim every day, Mr Scott,' Kate declared. 'As long as you don't mind her waiting until closing time, I promise to drive her home myself.'

Ryan remembered she'd tried to ignore him as much as she could when they worked for the same company, but their paths had crossed again, and he was ready to accept the situation. He had to admit that somehow he liked the idea.

'That won't be necessary. I'll pick her up.' He looked at the wall clock. 'I'll fetch her at roughly quarter to six. I expect after a couple of weeks she'll get fed up with it anyway.'

Kate kept her tone affable, but her eyes hardened. She tried not to glare at him.

'You don't want her to come here, do you?'

He stuck his hands in his jacket.

'No,' he replied emphatically. 'She doesn't need extra pocket money, and I don't think her parents would approve of her waiting on other people.'

The colour rose in Kate's cheeks.

'That is a snobbish remark. There's nothing wrong with waiting. Someone has to do it. We make someone else's day more enjoyable. Perhaps you should ask yourself why Kim wants to come. I realise it's not for the money. She's bored.

'She isn't used to her new school yet, and she's too intelligent to want to spend all her spare time watching television or with you. You should be pleased that she's interested in doing real work. It is a new experience.'

He listened, noted her eyes were the colour of pewter when she was angry, and forgot his objections.

'I assure you that I'm doing my best to accept this in a positive way, but she's my responsibility as long as my sister and her husband are away. I take my responsibilities seriously, and I want what's best for Kim. I'm not convinced that this is the best way for her to spend her spare time, that's all.'

He turned and delivered his parting words over his shoulder.

'Oh, the name is Ryan, and good luck with your café!'

Kate watched him as he went towards the door. He took lengthy determined strides. His slim chinos emphasised his long legs and his tall athletic physique.

The soft leather jacket with a navy sweatshirt peeping out underneath the collar looked what they were: expensive casual wear. Kate didn't understand why he unsettled her.

Kim waved her goodbyes and, clutching her jacket to her chest, hurried after Ryan.

Reluctant Phone Call

Nick whistled gently.

'What was that about? Neither of you seemed exactly delighted to see one another.'

Feeling annoyed with herself, because she hadn't been as friendly as she should have been, Kate frowned.

'He's my former divisional manager. In the hierarchy he was my boss, but I never had much to do with him.'

'Was he the one who fired you?'

'Nick, I fired myself. I don't know much about him and I take him as I find him. Knowing he was in charge presumably makes the chemistry between us skew whiff.'

Nick laughed.

'Sometimes women are attracted to power like moths to the light or, as in your case, put off. Perhaps he attracts you more than you care to admit?'

She slapped him gently with the tea cloth.

'Don't be silly!'

'Why not? It isn't like you to pounce on people and that's what you were doing. He was perfectly polite and civil until you started being nasty.'

Kate picked up the cloth and began wiping the counter.

'I wasn't nasty, just not very pleasant. Thank you, dear brother, for pointing out I should have been more diplomatic, but it's too late to show how gracious and courteous I can be. I don't suppose I'll see him in here very often, so don't give it a second thought.'

Nick laughed. He indicated towards a table with two women who were ready to pay.

'I'll be off. Despite everything, your first day was a howling success.' He kissed her on her cheek, grabbed his jacket, and disappeared.

Kate hurried over to collect money from the last stragglers. She then began to tidy the tables ready for the next day.

She glanced out of the window and tried to forget Ryan Scott. Apart from him, she was happy with her day.

Even the weather had been kind. As the late afternoon turned into early evening and threw long shadows along the almost deserted beach, she noticed some warmly dressed people were still walking their dogs. The fresh breezes were playing with their scarfs.

Perhaps tomorrow would be dry again. That would draw in more weekend visitors and it would be another busy day in Something's Brewing.

* * *

Sunday was just as good. Kim left as arranged at a quarter to six.

Kate didn't see Ryan Scott and wasn't sorry. She resisted the temptation to ask Kim about him, and waved Kim off with a cheery smile. Kim grinned back and patted her pocket with her well-earned money before she disappeared.

During the following week, Kate was

busy but found she could cope easily on her own. Several local people dropped in for coffee in the morning, and there were plenty of casual visitors to the beach in the afternoons, too.

The coffee machine was Italian, and was her most expensive investment. She didn't have the knack of making patterns on top of the frothy creamed coffee yet, and she wasn't as fast as a city coffee bar, but she would soon get the hang of it.

Kim called in almost every day on her lunch break. Kate warned her about absconding from school but Kim insisted that the upper sixth forms had more privileges, and the teachers turned a blind eye. She chatted about her school lessons and mentioned that the crowd Kate had seen her with that first day was still hassling her. They were now also making fun of her for working at Kate's café.

'It's a bit of a drag,' Kim declared, trying to sound unconcerned, 'but I try to avoid them if I can. If I meet one of them on their own, it's OK. When they're in a crowd I try to keep out of their way as much as I can.'

Kate was preparing an afternoon tea for someone. She concentrated on what she had to do, and tried to sound relaxed.

'I hoped things had improved for you by now. How long have you been there now?'

'Almost three months.'

'And it's not any better?'

'A bit. Some of the others at least talk to me and even let me join in. For some reason the ones that you saw that day seem to have it in for me. They shout abuse at me and push me around a bit if they get the chance.'

Kate was shocked.

'That's bad, Kim. You ought to tell your teacher or go to your headmaster and complain. Does your uncle know?'

'If the teachers or the headmaster get involved, they'll never let me forget it. Ryan might even blame me and tell me to make friends instead of being unsociable and hostile. I bet he'll tell me that when he went to school he never had problems like that.'

She looked at her watch.

'I've got to get back; two hours of French this afternoon. I like it, but I've got to be careful not to show I'm ahead of the others, otherwise they'll make my life a misery.' She picked up her bag and waved as she ran for the door.

Kate felt wretched. She was a nice kid, and there was no reason for anyone to dislike her. She even deliberately hid the fact that she was smarter.

As Kate made coffee, brewed tea, and served Monica's scones and cakes, she began to think about how she could help.

The bullying had to stop, but she couldn't think of a solution straight off. Kim didn't want to go to the teachers and she hadn't told Ryan because she thought he wouldn't understand.

* * *

Kate's parents called one afternoon to see her café. They were impressed and full of praise for Monica's cake. When they were leaving, her father threw his arms round her and gave her a hug.

'To be honest, Mum and I were sceptical when you told us you were giving up a good, secure job to open your own café, but you've done a great job. It looks classy. We can see you're happy and enjoying it. You can't buy that with money.'

Kate nodded.

'I don't regret a thing.'

He smiled.

'You know where we are if you need us.'

'I've always known that.'

* * *

Saturday came round quickly and Kate was more than satisfied with the way things were progressing. When Kim turned up, customers were already sitting at some of the tables.

The day was busy and Kate had to phone Monica for more scones and another cake. She turned up with warm scones, a Black Forest tart, and a plate of lemon tartlets decorated with raspberries.

Sunday was very busy again and thinking about the financial risks she'd taken, Kate relaxed a little.

She discovered from the occasional chat that some of the customers were locals, who were trying her out. They promised they would come back and she knew that was a good sign. She didn't want to rely solely on holiday visitors. She needed customers in the colder seasons, too.

Kim called in once or twice the following week. When she came on Thursday, Kate could see that she'd been crying.

Kate wasn't too busy so she brought her a cappuccino and a sandwich and sat down opposite.

'What's wrong, Kim? What's happened? You know you can tell me.'

Kim rubbed her hand over her cheeks and tried a weak smile.

'It's nothing important.'

'Come on, something's bothering you!'

Kim took tentative bites of her sandwich before she reluctantly answered.

'That stupid Roger Makepeace locked me in the lab after the chemistry lesson. It was my turn to clear up after the lesson. Usually there should be two of us, but my partner was ill and I told Mr Powell I'd manage. The others left, and I only noticed I couldn't get out when I'd finished. The lab is separate from the rest of the building, at the back.

'I had to wait until Mr Powell returned for the next lesson. The windows have safety wiring and I didn't want to break them to get out. When he came back I couldn't accuse anyone, because I couldn't prove who it was, and anyway, it would have made things worse.'

'How childish! Kids of your age don't usually do that sort of thing any more. Why do you think Roger did it, if you didn't see him?'

'He kept making faces during the history lesson afterwards and grinning. The rest of the crowd giggled and laughed when I passed them in the corridor later.'

'They're the same lot that I saw outside that first day?'

Looking more relaxed again, Kim grimaced.

'Yes, the same stupid bunch, and I don't know why they keep targeting me, but I suppose they get a kick out of it.'

A customer raised her hand for the bill, so Kate had to leave her for a moment. Kim was still drinking her cappuccino when Kate sat down again.

'Would you like me to help? I can talk to them, or to your teacher.'

Kim waved her hand.

'No, don't do anything, please. That would make things worse.' She changed the conversation and looked around. 'How's business?'

'Good. If every day was like this, I'd have no worries.'

Kim left in time for afternoon school

and while Kate was serving and clearing the tables she considered the best course of action. Finally, although she was very reluctant to contact him, she decided she had to phone Ryan Scott. He was responsible for Kim in her parents' absence.

She dialled the number for divisional headquarters and asked his secretary to put her through to him.

'Good morning, Kate. What can I do for you?' Kate decided that the sole reason why she felt like a breathless girl of eighteen was the friendliness in his voice.

'Good morning. I think I can do something for you.'

'You can do something for me?' He sounded intrigued.

'I'm all ears.'

Kate thought she could hear a hint of amusement in his voice. They weren't friends and here she was suggesting she could help.

'It's to do with Kim. She needs your support.'

'Kim?' His voice was more alert now. 'Has something happened? Some kind of accident? She doesn't work at your café during the week, does she? She ought to be in school.'

'She is in school.' Kate didn't mention Kim was skipping school lunch hours and visiting her at the café. 'It's about her school and what's going on.'

He sounded puzzled.

'Her school?'

Kate was exasperated.

'Haven't you noticed that something is bothering her?'

'No, I haven't. She seems happy enough. She hasn't mentioned any problems and I haven't noticed anything out of line, either. I check her grades now and then and they are above average.'

'School marks are not an indication if someone is happy or not.'

There was a moment's silence.

'Look, I have a conference scheduled in ten minutes. It sounds like we need to talk for longer than five. Can we postpone this till later?'

Before she could protest, he spoke again.

'I'm not trying to fend you off, I just haven't got the time for a lengthy telephone call just now. If you like, I'll call at the café on my way home, or before I drive to work tomorrow. I'll meet you some other place, at whatever time you suggest, if that doesn't suit.'

It didn't sound as if he were trying to avoid her, and he probably was busy. She conceded.

'I close the café at six, and I'm usually there every day for half an hour or so afterwards, clearing and preparing things for the next day. Would that suit you?'

'That would be perfect. This evening? I'll try to be on time. You have me worried and a little curious. See you later.'

'Yes, till later.' She disconnected and took a deep breath.

A Problem Shared

He arrived on time, just after six. Kate coloured slightly for some stupid reason as she unlocked the door and let him in. She led the way to a table.

'Would you like a coffee, or something else?'

He offered her an arresting smile and Kate could only muse that it was the first time he'd ever smiled directly at her. The smile changed his expression completely and made him look much younger.

'No coffee, thanks. I drink too much coffee all day long. A glass of milk or some water would be welcome if it's not too much bother.'

'Of course not.' Kate was glad to busy herself for a moment or two, and concentrate on something other than a pair of intelligent brown eyes surveying her from where he sat. She returned with milk and one of Monica's tartlets.

He eyed the cake.

'That looks tempting. Thanks. So, what's this all about? What is bothering Kim that I've missed?'

Kate explained, and he didn't interrupt until she finished.

'I realised you hadn't noticed and that Kim hasn't mentioned anything to you. I think you should try to intervene in some way if you can think of how to do it without making things worse. The situation is bothering her a lot. She was almost in tears when I talked to her the other day. Someone played a trick on her and they locked her in the chemistry lab.'

His fork halted in mid-air and he looked astonished. His eyes narrowed speculatively.

'I've certainly missed all this. She always seems happy at home. I must admit that it isn't easy to read a seventeen-year-old girl's mind.

'I didn't notice that anything was wrong.' He sighed. 'An uncle is no stand-in for a parent. I doubt whether she's mentioned anything to my sister, either. They talk to each other a couple of times a week on Skype.'

His close proximity made her stomach clench tight. She wondered why her pulse was all haywire.

I am not attracted to him, she told herself. Pull yourself together. She managed to steady her voice.

'The majority of teenagers keep troubles to themselves. They think they have to cope. Can you remember what it was like at that age?'

His eyes mellowed and he smiled.

'Yes, just about. You're right.' He looked thoughtful. 'I could go to the headmaster and complain, but I think I'll try a more personal approach first.'

Kate nodded.

'I suggested she should go to her form teacher or the headmaster, but she dismissed that idea outright. Would you like me to ask my brother what they do at his school?'

His brow wrinkled.

'Not yet. I need to be very diplomatic and make her admit that she's being mobbed, because that's what I call it. Then I'll worm some names out of her and try to collar them.

'I can drop her off at school one morning and she can point them out. I'll then try to talk a little sense into them, or threaten them if that doesn't work. I can always try to corner the parents, but I have to be careful or I'll make things worse. It could backfire. My last resort is to contact the school.'

He paused and his expression grew serious.

'I'm grateful that you've told me about this. My sister will kill me if Kim ends up a psychological wreck because I didn't take care of her. I guessed it wouldn't be easy for her to fit in, but I thought it was working out fine. I wonder why kids are so spiteful to each other.'

Kate shook her head. He considered her carefully for a moment.

'I'm glad Kim came here. You seem to attract people in need, don't you?

Probably because they know you won't push them away.'

Kate coloured.

'It doesn't cost anything to listen to other people. It's surprising how glad someone is just to talk about what's bothering them.'

'I seem to recall that giving someone a helping hand cost you your job,' he said as he stood up. 'Thank you for the milk and the cake — it was delicious. I'll keep in touch.'

He shoved the chair under the table, turned, and started walking towards the door.

Kate followed him and unlocked it. He held out his hand and she took it. It felt warm and comfortable.

'Thanks again. Goodnight.'

'You're welcome, Mr Scott. I hope you can somehow help Kim. I like her.'

He nodded.

'So do I. And the name is Ryan.'

Once he was outside, he flicked up the collar of his coat against the cold winds blowing in from the sea. With a last parting look, he lifted his hand and disappeared round the corner.

The seafront was deserted and the lamplights were coming on. Kate locked up and finished her preparations in the café for the next day.

She realised a short time later, when she was driving back to her flat, that since he'd left she'd spent more time thinking about the man, and how he'd looked, than the reason that had brought him to the café.

She reminded herself that she didn't have enough time to speculate about Ryan Scott, or any other man. Experience had told her they were just a bundle of trouble.

She straightened her shoulders. She intended to move out of her flat in a couple of weeks' time. The estate agent was certain he'd find a new buyer fast. It was in a decent part of the town in a quiet environment.

Nowadays she only had the evenings in the week to do any extra work. At the weekend, she was too tired.

She'd call at the DIY store for paint and start packing tonight. She'd start storing things in the small box-room as soon as it was ready. She didn't relish the idea of painting again, but she looked forward to living in the upstairs flat of the café.

* * *

Kate hoped to hear that Ryan had improved the situation when Kim showed up on Saturday morning. She had to stop herself asking questions. They were busy all day.

Mid-afternoon a crowd of school kids came past the shop and looked in through the window. They pointed in Kim's direction and fell about in hysterics, hooting with laughter. Kim noticed them and simply turned away.

Kate dried her hands on her apron and went outside.

'Hey, you lot, move on! You're bothering my customers.' Kate recognised Roger again.

'This is a free country, lady,' he shouted in a mocking tone. 'People are free to do what they like!'

His grey and white sweatshirt spelled out 'Yale' in white lettering. His bright sneakers with their massive soles added an inch or two to his height, and he thrust his hands demonstratively into his ripped jeans.

'That's true. Does it also mean I have the right to clout you round the earhole for being loutish?'

He stepped forward until his nose was right up to her face.

'Just try those tactics and my old man will come down on you like a ton of bricks.'

Kate's pulse increased and her mouth was dry. She didn't think he would actually do her physical harm, but you never knew. He was a potential candidate to be a nasty piece of work when he grew up.

Kate realised he was annoyed because she supported Kim. He wasn't used to opposition.

Staring him out and trying not to show the least concern, Kate spoke quietly and firmly.

'Either you stop your antics right now and move on, or I'll call the police and tell them you're making a public nuisance of yourselves in front of my premises.'

One of the girls in the straggle of kids alongside him groaned. She tossed her blonde curls and waved her crimson-tipped fingers at him.

'Oh, come on, Roger! Let's go. I couldn't care less if she's working there or not. I'm only glad I'm not and that I get enough pocket money to do something better with my time. She's welcome to it. Apart from anything else, my mother will kill me if word gets back to her that I was in the middle of a bunch of kids causing trouble.'

Kate noticed that some of her customers had come to stand in the doorway.

Some of the other kids started to murmur, too, saying it was time to go.

His eyes still blazing, Roger gave her a withering look and turned away. They immediately regrouped around him as they trailed off down towards the old wooden pier.

Kate watched them go. He turned again when they were a few yards away with a gesture of defiance in her direction. The other kids laughed and he grinned, clearly wallowing in their admiration as he swaggered on.

The Dream Coming True

One woman customer shook her head in despair.

'What are kids coming to these days? My mum and dad brought us up to be polite to our elders.'

An elderly man had come out with his wife. Leaning on a walking stick, he nodded.

'Lots of kids are decent and well-brought up, but when you see that lot, it's not hard to imagine that it won't be long before most of them will go off the rails and start doing real damage to themselves and others.'

Kim was standing outside, too, and looked at their departing figures.

'Sorry. They came here to annoy me but in school things are improving. I notice that some others in my class, ones who used to think that lot were great, don't any more. They don't laugh about things they do any more. I don't understand why they need to act like that in the first place. It gets them nowhere in the long run.'

Kate put her arm round the girl's shoulders briefly.

'I think Roger enjoys his commanding role so that he's able to impress girls and his other friends. He thinks his bullying tactics and picking on others is an effective way to impress others. What's he like in class?'

'To cover his own deficiencies he tells others that it's senseless to pay attention to the teachers, or to do the set homework. Most of the time he copies homework from his girlfriend, or anyone else who'll oblige, but the teachers aren't stupid.

'When we have tests, they see the difference. It's obvious that not everyone in class can get top grades, but at least most of us try. Roger doesn't. Trouble is, he's pulling the others down with him.'

'He won't get far with that attitude,'

Kate replied. 'If his marks are that bad all the time, he'll have to repeat the year. Without decent exams results, no-one gets anywhere these days. It looks like he's turning into a tearaway. Why do the girls in the group think he's so wonderful?'

'Susie, the blonde one, is too stupid to realise that although he acts cool and pretends to be a cut above the rest, he has a brain the size of a peahen. Susie is his girlfriend, but some of the other girls hope he'll dump her. I don't understand it, either; he must have qualities I've missed.'

'Well, I'm glad you see through him. I'm pleased to hear that at least some of your class have realised Roger and his crew are idiots.'

Kim nodded.

'I'm surprised to see them here today. In school they're ignoring me. It's lovely. Perhaps they've decided to pick on someone else.'

Kate laughed softly.

'Perhaps they've targeted me. Roger

needs to impress the others. He didn't like me telling him off the other day.' She brushed her hands on her apron. 'Let's get back to our customers.' She checked the room. 'Some of them are getting impatient.'

Back inside, Kate made sure that the customers who had come outside to support her had a cup of coffee and cake on the house.

As she busied herself, she decided Ryan Scott must have already done something to improve the situation. She wondered what it was.

Occasionally they heard bumps and some movement from upstairs.

'What's going on up there?' Kim asked. 'I thought the flat was empty.'

'Nick offered to help me today. He's painting the box-room, so that I can put some stuff there. You know that I'm selling my flat and moving upstairs? I didn't expect him this morning, but he insists on helping. When the box-room is finished, I'll be able to bring packed boxes with me every day.

'I'm going to start painting the living-room next. That's the biggest room, and then the kitchen and the bedroom.'

'I'll help if you like.'

Kate reached across and covered her hand.

'That's very kind, but you must concentrate on school during the week. You give up your weekends to help me in the teashop — that's enough at present. I reckon I can paint at least a wall a day.'

'Have you decided on colours?'

'I've got that all organised. I've written down what colour goes where, with its number. I gave Nick the list. That's why I don't need to keep checking on him. I've even double-checked by sticking the number and where it goes on the tubs of paint.'

'I bet he's thirsty. I'll take him something to drink.'

'He's got a flask of tea, but he's probably finished that by now. If you like, you can take him a piece of Black

Forest tart and find out if he needs anything else.' Kate reached into a drawer and put a key on the counter. 'That's the spare key to the flat.'

Kim nodded.

'I'll just serve that couple in the corner then I'll pop upstairs. I'm curious to see the flat. I've never been up there.'

Kate laughed softly.

'It's not bad. The living-room and the bedroom look out on to the beach. The kitchen, bathroom, and the box-room — the owner calls it a guest bedroom — looks out on to the back yard. I always wanted to live on the edge of the sea.'

'You won't have much time to enjoy anything if you continue to run the café all on your own.'

'Once everything is organised and I have an idea of the customer flow, I may find that I can afford to open up later in the day. In winter, it will be much quieter and perhaps I'll only need to open in the afternoon.

'In my free time, I'll be able to take

long walks on the beach or sit and watch the sea. I just want to earn enough to feel secure. I don't want to make a fortune.'

'And what happens if you get married. Have you got a boyfriend?'

Cutting a chocolate gateau into equal portions, Kate laughed.

'You're very curious today, aren't you? I'm doing something I always wanted to do. I don't know where it will end and at this moment I don't care much, either. The teashop is my dream. I don't have a boyfriend and I'm not looking for one. I presume if I did, I'd somehow manage to carry on.'

'Don't you like men?'

'Of course I do, well . . . I like the decent ones. The trouble is that the decent ones are hard to find. My last boyfriend was a catastrophe.'

Kim nodded.

'Men are often a drag, aren't they? Ryan wants to know all the time what I'm doing, where I'm going, who I'm meeting. I'm seventeen, I'm not a kid any more, but if you listened to him, you'd think I was five years old.'

Kate chuckled.

'I expect he feels very responsible. He's only trying to look after you. It would probably be better if you didn't wait for him to question you. Take the wind out of his sails, as the saying goes, and give him information before he asks!'

Kim looked thoughtful.

'I could give it a try, I suppose. I wanted to help someone with her homework last week and it was a fight to the death until he let me go. Lara is nice and she's good at most things, but she has trouble understanding maths and I offered to go through everything with her.'

Kate tilted her head.

'That's good of you. If you told Ryan about your plans, it won't stop him worrying, but it might mean he'd give you a bit more freedom.'

One of their customers lifted a hand.

'The table by the window wants

something. Perhaps you'd like to pop upstairs with the cake for Nick afterwards. It's quiet at the moment, but in half an hour or so I reckon we'll be busy again.' Kate looked at the cooling cabinet. 'I must phone Monica for more cakes and some extra scones for tomorrow. Sunday is always very busy and the weather forecast is good.'

Kim bustled off, and Kate mused there were still a lot of decent kids around after all.

* * *

When six o'clock arrived Kate was tired, and her feet were, too. She wasn't used to standing for most of the day, but she'd get used to it.

After Kim left and she'd cleared the café, she clattered upstairs. Nick was wrapping his brushes in plastic, so that they didn't need cleaning.

He looked up and grinned.

'Hi! I'm finished for the day, too.' He gestured with a wide sweep of his hand.

'I even managed to paint the window frame. It looks good, doesn't it?'

Kate looked around with pleasure.

'It's great. The colour brightens it up no end. I guessed it needed a cheerful colour because these rooms at the back of the flat are darker.'

He nodded.

'Luckily, I only needed to sand down some uneven bits here and there before I could paint.'

'Thanks for being such a brick. You've already helped me no end downstairs. I'll pay you back one day if you ever get round to redecorating your flat. I'll scrub the floor now, and lay Gran's Persian rug down in here tomorrow. It will be a perfect place to store my boxes.'

'You're welcome. I only do it because you're my favourite sister.'

She laughed.

'As I am your only one, that's not as flattering as it sounds.'

'I can't come tomorrow. I'm going to Leicester to the football match with

Duncan. It was hard to get tickets and I don't want to cry off.'

She touched his arm gently.

'You go and enjoy yourself. The fact that this room is finished is already a tremendous help.' She checked the time. 'I'll treat you to a pizza now, if you fancy one. There's a nice little Italian restaurant down a nearby side street.'

He shook his head.

'I just about have time to get home and have a shower before I meet someone to go to a performance by the local dramatic society.'

'Another time.' She kissed him briefly on his cheek. 'I'll just do the floor then it will have plenty of time to dry out during the night.'

Nick changed his paint-speckled T-shirt and picked up his coat.

'OK! Don't forget to lock the entrance door whenever you come up here. Once the sun disappears, the seafront is probably deserted. Don't give wrong-doers a chance.'

'Don't nag. I'll remember. I'll come

down with you to get a bucket and a scrubbing brush. You can't imagine how marvellous it is to know that at least one room is finished.'

She followed him and they went outside. The flat's entrance was right next door to the café. She waited for a moment until he disappeared from sight.

Kate spent another hour scrubbing and cleaning. Daylight had faded completely by the time she was ready to go. She stood for a moment looking out across the grey sea. There were still one or two people out walking their dogs.

Along the esplanade, everything was dark apart from the circles of light from the cast-iron lampposts. Her dream of living by the sea was coming true and she didn't intend to let any negative thoughts spoil that.

She looked at the windows of the café then up to the windows of the flat. She threw back her shoulders. It would work. She'd make it work.

Conflicting Emotions

Kate spent the evening packing boxes to take to her new flat the following day.

It was a struggle to get her gran's folded Persian rug into her car next morning, and even more of an effort to grapple her way up the stairs with it. It was heavy.

The planking in the box-room was dry. She'd varnish it later, but for now the room would be ideal as a storeroom.

She arranged the carpet. Its most prominent colours were red and dark blue. She stood, hands on hips and admired the result. She then carried up the boxes from her car parked in a side street just around the corner.

She checked the cans of paint she intended to use were all there from her list on the window-sill, and laid protective sheeting on the floor. She thought about which wall in the living-room she'd paint later.

Looking at her watch, she saw she didn't have any more time to do anything else. Holidaymakers might decide to have an early cup of coffee or a sandwich. She had to start the coffee machine and open up.

Kate could tell early on that it was going to be a busy day. The weather was fine and the morning mist over the sea had lifted long ago. Kate was glad when Kim arrived on time and Kim hurried to put on her apron and start serving as the café began to fill up.

Kate found it strange that some people seemed to love cake for their breakfast. She shrugged — there was no accounting for tastes. She'd started noting how much bread and other food items she used each day, so that she could make a more accurate estimate of what to order for which day. She had frozen bread and cakes as an emergency supply, but she wanted to have everything fresh if she could.

Monica's cakes were perfect and Kate heard how people praised them. She mused that sometimes fate chose unusual paths. If Monica hadn't lost her job, and if she hadn't decided to quit soon after, she wouldn't be standing in her own café today, and Monica wouldn't be in a more stable financial position.

* * *

The shop next door had a rotating stand of postcards, various beach equipment for children, and a stand of weekend papers and magazines outside on the esplanade.

Kate wondered if you needed a special licence to put tables outside. There was room for at least three outside the café and they wouldn't interfere with people walking along the front.

During the course of the day, she thought she heard several bumps upstairs, but there was no-one there and she was too busy to check.

Her landlord sauntered in halfway through the morning.

Gerald Hardwick looked around. Kate didn't particularly like him but he'd given her fair terms in the end. He was a grey-haired stocky man in his fifties who derived great pleasure from listening to his own jokes.

He came up to Kate at the counter and nodded.

'You've done a good job. The place is hardly recognisable. I always knew this place could be a little gold mine for the right person,' he said. 'If I'd known how much better it could look, I would have put up the rent.'

'But you would have had to clean and modernise first,' Kate couldn't help responding. 'It wouldn't have stood empty so long if you'd done that long ago.'

He laughed heartily.

'I inherited it. I want to earn money with the place, not invest in it. I've thought about selling it a couple of times, but the selling price never reached my expectations. Now that you've done it up, those prospects are much better.'

'Not unless I agree to cancel our agreement before the given date. My lawyer made sure that as a sitting tenant, it would be very difficult for you to evict me or revoke the agreement.'

He stroked his chin.

'Yes. I didn't pay much attention to all the small print when we signed the contract. Not that I'm complaining; I can see you've done a lot of work, but perhaps you'll go bust and you'll be glad to get out.'

'Don't rely on that,' Kate said. 'I've only just started, Mr Hardwick.'

'Gerald, please. We can forget the Mr Hardwick, can't we?' His mouth spread into a thin-lipped smile and he gave a brief shrug. 'Not knowing what the future will bring is always difficult.'

He looked at his watch. With a bland smile and a last glance around, he tipped his forehead.

'I'll be seeing you.

Kate wasn't sorry to see him leave. He was her landlord and as long as she paid her rent on time, there was no reason for him to keep calling. She hoped he wouldn't make a habit of it.

* * *

Kate was busy all day. Now and then she peeked through the window when serving one of the tables. For a second she thought again about the fact she was achieving her childhood dream and couldn't quite believe it was happening.

Only metres away the ocean was alive with constant motion. Every time the door opened, she smelled salt air and heard the babble of people on the esplanade out for the day.

Today the waves were the gentle kind that rolled up the beach like an overflowing bathtub.

She suddenly realised that this place was now her hometown, and her job had nothing to do with technology or gimmicks, she was just part of the coastal community.

By the time the golden light of the

late afternoon spilled across the floor, Kate and Kim were both glad the day was ending. The tables were almost empty and Kate started to clear things for the next day.

Kim was behind the counter, wryly eyeing the last stragglers.

'If they ask for another coffee, I'm going to tell them we're closing. It's already past six.'

Kate smiled.

'A lot of people lose track of time when they're with friends, but I agree. We have to draw the line somewhere. I'm glad people feel happy and comfortable, but if I start giving in every time someone hasn't quite finished their coffee or their conversation, I'll be here until seven or eight every day. I don't like shoving people out, but opening times are from nine till six.'

'Have you brought any stuff from your old flat with you today?' Kim asked.

'Yes, a couple of boxes of things and my gran's old carpet. I've laid the carpet and carried the boxes upstairs already. Nick finished painting the box-room for me yesterday and I cleaned it before I went home. I intend to paint one of the sitting-room walls before I go home today. I'll get it done wall by wall.'

'Why don't you go up there now?' Kim suggested. 'I'll lock up and bring you the key before I go.'

Despite feeling tired, Kate was looking forward to painting. She hurried upstairs and opened the door. The breath caught in her lungs when she saw Ryan Scott with a paintbrush in his hands.

One wall facing the door was finished and its pale yellow colour already radiated light through the rest of the room. He'd also almost finished the second wall.

She hesitated on the threshold, blinking with bafflement. He saw her confusion and his features relaxed into a smile of amusement.

'Yes, it's me, and I hope I've got the colours right. Kim told me you'd made a list of what goes where, and you even noted the colour numbers on the tins quite clearly, so I think I've used the right ones.'

With her expression still slightly dazed, she finally managed to speak.

'What are you doing here?'

'Helping, I hope. I thought it might be a good way of thanking you for caring about Kim's troubles in school.'

Under his steady scrutiny, she needed a moment to gather her thoughts. She swallowed and found her voice again.

'There was no reason to thank me for anything. I only talked to her. She's very sensible and a good worker, too. She says things are better now.'

He considered her for a moment.

'Kim told me about your confrontation the other day with the group of kids outside your café. As Kim described it, they were pretty aggressive.'

Kate gestured around the room.

'That doesn't mean you had to spend your spare time doing this. How did you get in? Did Kim slip you the spare key from downstairs?'

He laughed softly and Kate experienced strange and disquieting feelings running through her brain.

'Yes. I presumed you'd refuse outright if I asked, so Kim suggested I just did it without asking. As you'd already decided on the colours and efficiently listed everything, I hoped you'd appreciate a little help.'

Kate took a deep breath and glanced at the sections he'd finished. She nodded.

'Yes, exactly right. It looks good. Thank you. Though I'm sure you have better things to do on a Sunday than painting someone else's flat.'

He ran his free hand through his hair and Kate wondered if he'd get paint on it.

'I haven't done anything like this since my student days. It started me thinking how long ago that was.'

To Kate's way of thinking, Ryan Scott's spontaneous help was out of character, but she wasn't in a position to question it. She didn't like being beholden to him, either, but for some strange reason he seemed to think he had to repay her.

His voice sent a ripple of awareness through her as he continued.

'I like your flat. It's very compact and great for a single person. The view from these windows is unbeatable.'

She nodded.

'It was one of the reasons I thought it was the ideal place for me. I always wanted to live near the sea, and I always wanted to run a teashop. When the estate agent suggested this building, I knew straight away this was it.'

His brilliant eyes twinkled.

'Well, you've certainly hit the mark, haven't you? Not many people get around to doing what they've always dreamed of.'

'Kim told me you live on the other side of the town?'

He nodded.

'I was lucky enough to buy a bungalow someone built in the twenties. Nowadays new building permission round that area is nil. It's not very far from the cliff path in its own plot of land, and there are only a couple of other houses in the vicinity.

'It used to belong to a retired general who sold it when his wife died. I gutted most of the inside and reorganised it. I managed to persuade the planning office to allow me to build a conservatory out the back, and that makes the sitting-room a lot more spacious.

'A landscape gardener re-planned the surround in such a way that it blends in. He did a good job because from the road you just think it's only a little more tamed than the rest of the vicinity.' He tilted his head and smiled.

'It is also labour saving,' he continued, 'which is very good as far as I'm concerned. From the bungalow you look past boulders and grasses and various heathers to the ocean beyond.'

The atmosphere relaxed between them.

'Most people love the idea of a home near the sea, but I bet it's pretty stormy on top of the cliff in winter, isn't it?' Kate asked. 'I would have thought you'd prefer to live in the middle of a bustling town.'

She saw an unmistakable flash of amusement on Ryan's face.

'True, it's pretty wild some days, but there's a special fascination about storms. The route for our cars is very basic. The footpath going up starts at the end of the esplanade.

'I've always loved the sea, and I have a sailing boat moored in a nearby harbour. I enjoy sailing whenever time allows and I like this community. It's a complete contrast to the demands of the company.'

He met her glance and held it.

'I am not the brittle, uncaring businessman with no hobbies and no feelings that you seem to believe I am.'

She felt conflicting emotions. He was more approachable and likeable than she'd hitherto surmised. The mere fact that he'd taken on his sister's daughter for a while showed he had a side to his character that wasn't immediately evident.

'And do you have a hidden dream like me and my café? One that has nothing to do with your work?'

He laughed softly.

'I'd love to sail around the world one day. Is that good enough?'

Heat stole into her face and she nodded.

'You'll do it one day, I'm sure.'

He smiled again and her pulse increased.

'If the time is ever right, I might.'

An Unexpected Kiss

Kim interrupted them when she burst in, her face split into a wide grin. She looked around.

'Wow! A bit of decent paint makes all the difference, doesn't it?'

Kate was glad to move her attention.

'Kim, I don't know if I should yell at you or not. You arranged it behind my back and pinched my key, too.'

Kim chuckled.

'I talked to Ryan and I knew if Ryan asked if he could help you wouldn't take it, so I told him he'd have to play a bit of cloak and dagger if he really wanted to help.'

'Well, it was kind of you both, but not necessary.'

'Are you hungry?' Kim asked Ryan. 'There are a couple of tasty sandwiches left over. You are going to finish that wall, I hope, before you decide to quit for the day.'

Kate started to protest, but Ryan just held up his hand and chuckled.

'Get the sandwiches, you brat, and a cup of coffee.' Turning to Kate with a grin, he added, 'I intended to finish the wall anyway so don't give it a second thought.'

Kim hurried out and, feeling flustered, Kate concentrated hard and looked at the wall he'd finished.

'It looks great! Just as I imagined. I can't thank you enough. I'll carry on now and finish another wall before the light fades and I'll be able to finish the whole room off tomorrow.'

He brushed her thanks aside.

'I'm pleased that I could help. I can't come tomorrow, I'm afraid. I have a meeting in Leeds first thing and won't be back until quite late, but if I can help in any other way you only have to ask. I usually have the weekends free.'

With heightened colour and feeling like a star-struck teenager, she shook her head.

'That's good of you. My brother is

coming down to help next weekend and bringing a friend who is an electrician. I want to get the kitchen finished before then. They're going to fix my kitchen and sort out the electric and plumbing connections. Your help today gives me more leeway to get things ready in time.'

'And when will you make your final move — your furniture and the like?'

'All going well, the weekend after.'

He eyed her silently.

'Good!'

He looked remarkably tidy, and even attractive, in working jeans and a washed-out shirt. There weren't many misplaced smudges or spots of paint on him, and she wondered how he managed that. She seemed to get paint specks everywhere, including in her hair.

'I'll start to paint the next wall,' she offered, 'if you insist on finishing that one, or I'll finish it off if you like. You've done enough. You'll be glad to go home.'

'I always finish what I start.' He dipped the paintbrush in the tin and turned back to the wall. 'It won't take long. By the way, I don't think it's a good idea to leave your spare key in the shop. Someone might notice and pinch it. There's not much to steal up here at present, but that will change. Leave it with someone you trust. Don't look for a convenient hiding place nearby; thieves know where to look.'

She busied herself with laying the protective sheeting then looked across at him.

'You're as bad as my brother. Anyone would think I was moving into an area of thieves and gangsters.'

He smiled and shrugged while moving the brush in controlled swipes.

'This is a decent place, but you never know these days. Ah! The welcome rattle of china. Kim is on her way. I'm parched!' He continued painting with strong, steady strokes again.

Kate popped into the adjoining room and changed into an old top and a pair of washed-out, shabby jeans. Wrapping a scarf around her head, she returned to the sitting-room and found Ryan sitting next to Kim. They were both leaning against an untouched wall and he was munching on some sandwiches. He looked up.

'Very attractive!'

Kate coloured and realised he wasn't being sarcastic. He was being friendly. She couldn't understand why she couldn't completely relax in his company. She would have retaliated with a suitable flippant remark if Nick or Duncan had tried to provoke or tease her in a similar way.

He wasn't her boss any more and he'd come voluntarily today. She knew she should shelve her preconceptions about him. He'd done something about Kim's problems in school and he was generous with his help, but she still found it difficult to be obliged to Ryan Scott for anything.

She moved to her painting area with quick strides and arranged the tins and brushes, checking for cobwebs and dust before she began to paint.

Kim and Ryan were talking quietly, and Kate tried to shut out their conversation. A few minutes later, Ryan came to his feet in one effortless movement and held out his hand to help Kim. He went back to finish his section.

Kim broke the silence.

'I've cleared up downstairs. I'll take the tray back. Anything else you'd like me to do?'

Kate looked up and smiled at her.

'No, thanks. Just make sure that I've shut off the coffee machine. I'm not sure if I did when I left.'

Kim balanced the tray and skipped towards the door.

'Will do! I'll be back in a minute.' She looked across at her uncle. 'Are you really almost finished? I can always walk home. I'll just get in the way doing nothing here.'

He laughed.

'No! By the time you're back, I'll be

ready. It's not a good idea for you to use the cliff path on your own at this time of day. We'll go home together.'

Kim pouted a little.

'Ryan, I am not a baby.'

'No, but I'm responsible, and I don't see why you should take unnecessary risks. Argue with your parents, not with me.'

Tossing her ponytail, Kim left.

Kate managed to sound quite normal.

'It isn't very easy sometimes, is it? Teenagers of that age are often at a rebellious stage in their lives, and on top of that you are not her father.'

He rubbed his hands together.

'True, but funnily enough, in a way I think she finds it's easier to accept things I say than if it came from her dad. With me, it's probably just a case of her testing her strength. I have a different standing. I'm a bit younger than her dad is, too, so that helps a bit. On the whole, she's a good kid.' He stood up, put the lid on his paint tin, clapped his hands again, and came closer. 'Well, that's it. If you're sure I can't do any more tonight.'

'I'm sure.'

He studied her and nodded. He looked around.

'This colour looks good on the walls — and on you. I wish I had a camera.' Unexpectedly, he reached forward and touched the tip of her nose with his finger. It came away covered in pale yellow paint. A smile lit up his face.

Kate felt suddenly self-conscious and aware of the confines of the small room. Ryan was too close and she held her breath for a long moment.

He slipped his arms round her shoulders and it felt wonderful; he felt warm and safe. His kiss was sweet but it quickly turned into something more thrilling. She was startled. She reminded herself they were both single and it had no special meaning.

For a moment or two rational thoughts fled, but it was no good — seconds later, she surfaced and focused her thoughts.

She stepped back. His gaze held hers.

His eyes were lustrous like rich mahogany.

She heard his questioning tone.

'Was that so shocking?'

She opened her mouth then shut it again.

'No, of course not,' she finally managed. 'Nothing to do with you. It was just unexpected. My last boyfriend left me disillusioned. I don't ever intend to rush into another relationship again.' Her eyes met his. 'I thought I knew him, but I didn't.'

'And you're going to let it influence you for the rest of your life? Sometimes unexpected things happen. Just relax and let fate decide.'

Her colour mounted.

'I don't suppose anyone has ever let you down in the same way, otherwise you'd understand better. I don't intend to put it down to experience, forget it, and wait for the next prince to come along on his white steed. Bad experiences do colour your attitude.'

Kate's thoughts steadied. Right now, she definitely didn't want another meaningless affair — especially with someone who'd been her former boss. A light-hearted flippant relationship might suit him, but she'd always wanted commitment. He was probably looking for someone to fill the gap in his present lifestyle and she was around and unattached.

She tensed. In the space of seconds, her mood had changed from good-natured assent to uncomfortable caution. She didn't need a man in her life at present, especially one like Ryan Scott.

He stood with his hands in his pockets, staring at her silently. Whenever she looked at him the harder she tried to ignore him, and the more she wished she knew more about him, and that confused her.

She tried to rub off the offending paint with the back of her hand, and only succeeded in smearing it even more. A drip from her own paintbrush plopped on to her arm and the tension between them lessened as he followed its trail and laughed softly.

'If you carry on like that, in a few hours' time you're going to look like an alien.'

Without another word, he turned on his heel and went towards the door. He looked back at her and frowned.

'Don't base your judgement on stupid people. Be grateful that you found out in time. He must have been a very stupid man.'

He went down the stairs whistling 'You Are The Sunshine Of My Life'. The tune drifted back and she felt very mixed up. It was just a brief kiss. The mere touch of his lips had confused her completely.

She ran her fingers over her lips and tried to remind herself that she didn't even like the man much.

She was cleaning the paint off her face when Kim reappeared with the key in her hand.

'I've locked up. I'll leave it here on the window-sill. I'll see you next Saturday at the latest.'

Kate smiled.

'I might not see you next Saturday or the one after. I'm hoping to sort the kitchen out this Saturday and move the bigger bits and pieces of my furniture the following week, if my brother has time. If I can't be in the café, Monica says she'll come in to help out for the day.'

Kim looked a little wary.

'Will she bring her little boy? If he's under our feet all day, it'll be a drag. There isn't much space for a kid to play or run around.'

Kate shook her head.

'Don't worry about that. If she comes, she'll leave Tim with her parents for the day. You'll get on with Monica, I'm sure. She doesn't just make delicious cake; she's very easy-going. Like you, she's a treasure, and you are both helping me to make a great start!'

Kim grinned.

'Oh, go on with you! I'm only after the money! Ryan is waiting. I must go or he'll start moaning again.' She whirled round and disappeared from sight.

Silence descended, and Kate could let her thoughts wander as she painted. She just wished they didn't wander so often in the direction of Ryan Scott.

Blossoming Romance

The following week was uneventful. There was a steady trickle of customers every day, and the numbers increased noticeably in the afternoon, especially whenever the sun appeared.

Kate was glad to note that local people seemed to be using the café increasingly as a meeting place. They came for a quick chat and a cup of coffee, and some people seemed to think it was a neutral place to have a quick business discussion.

Gerald Hardwick called again one afternoon. He declared he just happened to be in the vicinity and popped in for a coffee. Standing at the counter, Kate served him but didn't like the way he was looking around. She didn't like him 'dropping in' and she didn't particularly like him, either, but had to be polite because he was a customer like anyone else.

She'd finished the living-room and transported more boxes every day when she came to work. She now had to pile them around the edges of the living-room, too. After removing the horrible wallpaper in the kitchen, she re-papered it with lining paper, and painted it in pale green.

On Saturday, Nick and Duncan planned to pick up her kitchen units from her flat in a builder's van that Duncan had borrowed from his boss. For a change, they were punctual.

They shared a quick breakfast before they started to dismantle the sink connections and disconnect the cooker. By 11 o'clock, several units were loaded and ready for transport.

Unloading was a bit more exhausting, because the stairs to her new home were narrow and there was hardly any room to negotiate round the slight bend at the top.

After another short break when Monica supplied them with coffee and sandwiches from downstairs, the two men fetched the remaining units and began figuring out how best to reposition things.

They connected the plumbing and by mid-afternoon the kitchen was finished and all three of them looked proudly at the result.

Nick threw his arm round her shoulder.

'Well, there you are, sis! I think we did a good job. No gaps anywhere and you can now use the sink and the cooker.'

Kate beamed at him.

'It's fantastic!'

Duncan moved closer and pointed to his cheek.

'What about me? Don't I deserve a peck?'

Kate obliged and the two men started to collect Duncan's tools.

Nick indicated the spare unit.

'What are you going to do with that?'

She shrugged.

'Don't know yet. Leave it. If I can't think of a suitable place, I'll break it up and take it to the dump.'

The two men left and Kate listened to them clattering down the stairs, and then silence descended in the flat.

Kate admired the little kitchen and reluctantly left it all to join the two women in the café downstairs. It wasn't long until closing time, but she could at least give them a chance to leave a little earlier if they wanted to.

Brushing down her jeans and long-sleeved T-shirt, she smiled at them both, busy behind the counter, and grabbed one of the aprons from its hook.

Kim and Monica were already beginning to clear up, ready for tomorrow. There were still a couple of customers sitting at the tables, and they looked like they'd already been there a while.

'I can only say thanks,' Kate said.

Kim nodded and Monica smiled. They both hurried to assure her that they'd enjoyed helping her out.

'What was it like today? Lots of customers?'

Monica pushed a strand of hair from her face.

'A steady stream all day. The weather meant that visitors were taking advantage of the weather to come to the beach. When they see your sign, they realise they're longing for coffee and cake!'

Kate looked out of the windows.

'That's one thing I am also looking forward to. There's too much to do upstairs in the flat at the moment, but as soon as I can, I'll let the sea breezes blow the cobwebs from my brain every day after work.'

Kim made a face.

'I don't like the wind much and I've never understood this passion for walking along the shore. Are you sure you haven't been indoctrinated by all the romantic films we see all the time?'

Kate started to rearrange the items on the counter.

'I've always loved the wind, even when I lived inland. In wintertime, too. When you're properly dressed, the cold doesn't matter. Hey, you two, with my everlasting thanks, why don't you get your things and go home?'

'If you're sure?' Monica asked. 'I promised to give Nick a lift.' She started to remove her apron. 'They came in to say goodbye and as I'm going past Nick's place on the way to fetch Timmy, I told him to wait for me. It saves Duncan making a detour. He has to return the van to the depot before he can go home.'

Kate looked around.

'Where is Nick?'

Monica pointed outside. He was sprawled on one of the benches overlooking the beach and looking out to sea. Kate nodded. She turned to Kim.

'Are you ready to go, Kim? Is your uncle going to pick you up?'

'No, I persuaded him that the shortcut up the cliff path is still busy at this time of day.'

Kate laughed.

'Do you have to phone to warn him you're on your way?'

Kim's eyes sparkled.

'How did you guess? I have to text

him. He didn't get in till quite late last night. I think he was glad I was out of the way for a couple of hours!'

'Are you on your own sometimes overnight?'

She shook her head.

'Are you kidding? His home help stays if he has to go somewhere. She doesn't mind. It's all extra money. I'm not a kid any more, but it makes no difference. He keeps telling me to be careful.'

'How much do those people over there need to pay?'

'Two coffees, two sandwiches and an extra cappuccino.'

'OK.' She flicked her hands in the direction of the door. 'Shoo! Off you go!'

Kate checked her watch. She would be able to close in less than an hour then she'd wash out the kitchen units and touch up the paintwork before she left. After work tomorrow, she could start to unpack some boxes with kitchen stuff in them. Things were taking shape at last. She busied herself with keeping her eye on the last customers and getting ready for tomorrow.

She took a cake out of the deep freezer. She'd forgotten to mention to Monica that she needed more cake. Monica had done enough for one day; she wouldn't bother her with orders for baking this evening. Tomorrow was early enough.

Glancing out of the window, she saw Monica and Nick deep in conversation as they walked side by side. Nick was leaning towards her and Monica looked very relaxed in his company.

They disappeared round the corner to where Monica had parked her car. It started Kate thinking again.

* * *

Even by the following week, the flat was still a mess because there were boxes stacked everywhere. Her old flat looked just as bad, because it was half-empty, but the kitchen in her new home was functioning and a lot of her kitchen paraphernalia was already in place.

On Friday evening, Nick phoned. Duncan had broken two fingers and wouldn't be able to carry anything. She wondered how to replace him. It was almost impossible at such short notice.

She shrugged. She'd do her best, but the heavier objects, like her sofas, or chest of drawers, needed muscle power. If she took her time and they rested things now and then, they'd manage, even though there was a slight turn at the top of the stairs.

Late that afternoon, she phoned Kim.

'Kim, I forgot to mention that Monica is coming again tomorrow to help in the café. I'm moving in upstairs.'

'OK. Who's helping?'

'It's just me and Nick. Duncan was going to help, but he's broken a couple of fingers, so he is out of the running. We can still borrow his company van, although he has to drive it — otherwise his boss wouldn't let us have it.'

Kim was silent for a moment.

'Do you have a lot of heavy stuff?'

'Not that much. We'll survive. I don't want to cancel. I don't suppose Duncan can persuade his boss to keep lending us the van. I want to get it finished. Nick's given up enough of his time already.'

'Don't you know anyone else who could help?'

'I know a couple of people who I'd normally ask, but it's such short notice. Everyone generally has fixed plans for the weekend. We'll manage somehow.'

'Hmm! Sounds like a pretty exhausting job to me. I remember the last time my parents moved. It was chaos. My mum and dad shouted at me, and at each other, all day long.'

Kate laughed.

'Well, I don't expect to shout at anyone. Your move was a whole house, or at least a much bigger flat. The things I want are just too big for me to manage on my own in my car.'

'Like?'

'My couch, some chairs, some book-shelves, tables, my bed, and the wardrobe.'

'Well, rather you than me. I'd rather spend time waiting on old ladies in the café.'

Kate chuckled.

'So would I, but after tomorrow the worst is over. Then I only have to arrange it into a decent state.'

Making a Move

Saturday dawned. It was cold but dry. Kate looked out of the window as she put crockery on the table. She was grateful that at least the weather wouldn't make things more unpleasant.

She'd bought bread rolls and coffee was brewing. When the doorbell rang, she looked at her watch and was surprised. For once Nick was very punctual.

She pressed the button to open the door downstairs and left the flat door open before she went to pour coffee into vacuum flasks and the rest into a coffee pot.

She turned, smiling, when she heard the door close. The shock on her face must have been visible when Ryan stood considering her.

'Yes, it's me.'

Her throat was as dry as sandpaper, but after a second, she finally managed to speak.

'Ryan! What are you doing here?'

'Kim told me you needed an extra hand.'

Still completely confused, Kate brushed some loose strands of hair out of her face and hoped she sounded halfway normal.

'That's true, but I'm sure you have something better to do with your time this morning. It's my problem, not yours. I'll manage with my brother's help.'

His brown eyes twinkled and a wicked grin indicated what he was thinking.

'Don't be silly. Grab my help as long as you can. If you don't, you'll end up with a slipped disc and have to close your café for a week.'

Even though he was only wearing a run-of-the-mill long-sleeved grey polo shirt, dark jeans, comfortable sneakers, and a leather biker jacket, he still managed to look classy. Still lost for words a second later, she stuck her hands into the pocket of her jeans and took a deep breath.

'I don't know what to say.'

'Then don't say anything.' Taking off his jacket, Ryan looked at the table. 'I see you've made coffee. That would be very welcome. I haven't had any breakfast this morning.'

Pulling herself together, Kate gestured with her hand.

'Please, help yourself. There's cheese, jam and cooked ham. Not much else I'm afraid, because I haven't got a cooker here any more.'

He looked relaxed and reached for a roll.

'This is fine. More than I usually have.'

Trying to return to normality, she slipped into the opposite chair and lifted the coffee pot questioningly. He nodded and she poured him a cup.

'Don't you usually have breakfast?' she asked.

'It depends how pushed I am for time.'

Kate nodded understandingly and felt more at ease.

'When I'm away I have the bonus of

a hotel breakfast,' he added, then buttered his roll, covered it with a slice of cheese, and took a generous bite.

Kate poured herself a cup of coffee, rested her elbows on the table, and cradled the cup between her hands. Sharing an early morning breakfast with Ryan Scott had something far too intimate about it. She pushed the thought aside.

'Don't you mind? Having to travel around all the time?'

He shrugged.

'I don't, not that much. It's part of the job. If I reach the next step in the hierarchy at divisional headquarters, I'll be more fixed and permanent. After that, any further promotion would mean moving to London, and I'm not sure I want to do that.'

She reached out and buttered a piece of toast.

'You like your job?'

'Yes, otherwise I wouldn't do it. I like the variety and the chance it gives me to meet so many people.'

'But it isn't all roses, is it?'

'No. Sometimes I have to make difficult decisions about people, or things that happen, but I make it a rule to do it as impartially and humanely as I possibly can. I had to close down one of our shops recently, and that was hard because it was in an area where jobs were rare anyway.'

'I'd hate to be the cause of someone else's misfortune,' Kate commented.

He stretched his arms above his head.

'Well, at least I try to appreciate what my decision will mean for other people in the district because I'm also a local inhabitant. If someone from London did my job they wouldn't care so much, because they're not emotionally involved.' He reached for his cup. 'I do my best, Kate.'

She nodded and felt a sudden sympathy for him. She'd never considered what it must be like in his position when he had to make unpopular decisions.

As she looked across the table, she

experienced a confusing mixture of emotions. She didn't want to like him, but he dizzied her senses. There was more to him than a figure in a stiff business suit.

He broke into a leisurely smile and she found herself returning it. The doorbell interrupted them. She hurried downstairs to let the other two men in.

Nick breezed in with Duncan at his heels. He hugged her briefly.

'Have you got something to eat? I'm hungry and no-one can do work on an empty stomach.' He noticed Ryan sitting at the table. 'Who do we have here? Could it be that my prayers have been answered and someone else has volunteered to help?'

Ryan nodded and held out his hand. 'Morning! We meet again. My niece told me about Kate's predicament last night, and I thought another pair of hands might come in useful.'

'Your niece?'

'Kim. She's working in the café for Kate at the weekends. She's there this morning with . . . ' He looked at Kate for more information.

'Monica,' Kate supplied.

Straddling one of the chairs, Nick reached forward for a bread roll and nodded.

'Yes, Monica mentioned that she was coming in again.'

'Delighted that we have another pair of hands,' Nick said to Ryan. 'Duncan has managed to sidestep the work again.'

After kissing Kate on her cheek, Duncan joined the other two at the table and protested.

'Don't keep on! It wasn't my fault. My buddy sloped his chisel in the wrong direction and I didn't move my hand out of the way fast enough.'

Ryan made a suitable expression.

'Ouch!' he exclaimed.

'Anyway, it's put me out of action on the rugby pitch for a couple of weeks and that's the real catastrophe. The scrum will fall apart without me.'

Kate grinned and joined them.

'Duncan, there are more important

things in this world than rugby!'

'Not many! Although if I had to make a list, you'd come a close second.' He slipped his arm round her shoulder and hugged her for a moment.

'Stop flattering. Sit down, and eat! And remember you've come to help me move — I hope I don't have to listen to rugby statistics all day.'

Despite her warning, the conversation soon centred on rugby and the positions of the local teams in the tables. Ryan admitted he hadn't played rugby since he left school, but knew enough about the game to take part in the conversation.

'Are you into other sports?' Nick asked Ryan.

'I sail whenever I have the time.'

'You sail? Do you have your own boat?'

'Yes, it's second-hand and not very big, but it suits me fine.'

Nick nodded.

'I did a sailing course once when I was a kid, but a boat is an expensive undertaking unless you use it regularly.'

Ryan nodded.

'Agreed. My uncle always had a boat and passed his enthusiasm for the sea on to me. If you'd like a trip, just say the word. You, too, Duncan, of course.'

Nick nodded.

'Sounds good. Perhaps I'll take you up on that during the school holidays!'

'Do.'

Kate felt a slight sense of irritation that Ryan hadn't included her in the invitation. She busied herself with clearing the table.

'How about you lot doing something?'

Nick got up.

'Right! Let's make a start loading the van. If we're lucky, we'll do it all in two runs. The van isn't very big, so we'll have to see how things go.'

Ryan slipped his jacket over the back of a chair and followed Nick into the bedroom.

Kate had guessed that Duncan would feel left out and useless. With his injured hand, he wasn't going to be able to help much.

She'd purposely left some bookshelves full of books.

'Duncan, if you want something to do, will you pack those books, please? I'm going to carry some of the smaller boxes downstairs so that Nick and Ryan can use them to fill any spaces in the van.'

Although Kate tried to keep out of the way whenever the men handled the heavier bits of furniture, she couldn't help noticing how the outline of Ryan's shoulders strained against the fabric of his shirt, or how his thick brown hair fell forward on to his forehead. She had a stupid urge to push it back into place.

Kate had to admit her preconceptions about him hadn't been entirely fair. He took his responsibility about Kim seriously, had offered Kate spontaneous help, and evidently tried to avoid unnecessary hardship for employees. All that put him in another light.

They'd stopped for a short break

after the first van load, and Monica supplied them with hot soup she'd brought with her, and sandwiches from the café.

By early afternoon, the second van load was unpacked and the furniture was in position.

Kate sighed with relief. She'd made it. Apart from cleaning her old flat before the estate agent inspected and measured, she could forget it and concentrate on her new home.

Not having to travel back and forth every day would make a big difference. Waking to the sound of the sea would be a dream come true.

Kate looked around at her helpers who were sitting around on some of the unpacked boxes.

'I'll take you all out for a thank-you meal one evening. I'm so grateful.'

Nick stood up, putting his hands in the small of his back and stretching.

'Good idea, sis. I need to recover first. Come on, Duncan. Drive me back to your yard so that I can pick up my car. If we're lucky we'll catch the sports show. I've a pile of marking to do before Monday, but I can't face an exercise book tonight.'

Duncan reluctantly got to his feet.

'See you, Kate.'

'Yes, and thanks again. Even with broken fingers you were a great help, and please thank your boss for the use of his van.'

The two of them clattered down the stairs and the sound of their footsteps faded away. Ryan got to his feet.

'I suppose it's time for me to go, too.' He looked at his watch. 'It's almost time for them to close up downstairs, so I may as well wait for Kim, if you don't mind.'

'No, of course not.' She felt strangely nervous now that they were on their own again. 'I ought to go down and take over, but it's not worth bothering at this time and I look a sight.'

He stuck his hands in his pockets and looked her in the eyes.

'You look just fine to me.'

'I didn't realise the lighting in here was that bad,' she remarked, colouring.

For a moment she was lost for words.

'Thank you so much for helping today. For everything,' she finally said with a frog in her throat.

His brown eyes twinkled.

'You're welcome, and don't try moving heavy bits of furniture on your own. You have our phone number and it would only take a couple of minutes for me to pop down to help.'

The clatter of feet on the stairs announced Kim. She knocked and came in. Looking around, she grimaced.

'There's even more chaos than before!'

Kate smiled.

'Yes, but I'm in! And don't worry about the chaos. In a week or so, it'll look like a palace. I take it that you've come to collect your uncle?'

'Yes, I hope he's ready to drive me home. We've closed up and prepared things for tomorrow. Monica will bring the key in a couple of minutes. See you tomorrow.'

Kate nodded. She looked at Ryan.

'Herewith I return your uncle to your care — and order you not to annoy him any more this evening. He's done a great job.'

Kim turned away.

'So have I, so we'll have to be kind to each other, won't we?' She opened the door and disappeared.

Ryan smiled as he slung his jacket over his shoulder.

'She's full of beans.' He drew closer and as he stood alongside her, for some unexplainable reason she found it hard to breathe.

They stared silently at each other for a moment before he leaned forward and kissed her cheek.

'Night, Kate. Have an early night. I'll be seeing you!'

As she stared at the closed door, Kate reached up and touched her cheek. He didn't mean anything special by touching her with his lips fleetingly, but it awakened feelings she couldn't ignore.

No-one Special

The following day was very busy. Sundays were turning into her busiest day. At a quiet moment, she phoned Monica to order some more cakes and thanked her again for her help.

'I enjoyed doing something different. I love Timmy, but it's nice to have a break from building unrecognisable things with Lego, or reading the same story for the hundredth time!'

Kate teased her.

'I must say, your time in my café is changing your attitude.'

'Nick and I were talking the other day about the various characters who wander in and out of your café. I like your brother. He's very down to earth, and I bet he's a good teacher. He listens to people and he likes children.'

'Nick seldom takes a dislike to anyone. Teaching isn't an easy job.'

'No, I'm sure you're right there. I'll make those cakes tomorrow morning and bring them round when Timmy is in nursery.'

'Everyone is wild about your cakes. People often ask me where they come from, but I don't tell them or you'd be overrun with orders from my customers — and my competitors.'

Monica chuckled.

'I'm glad. Thanks for ringing, Kate. See you tomorrow.'

* * *

Kim was always cheerful and helpful. It meant she often went home with a generous amount of tips, as well as what Kate paid her. As the working day finished, they chatted as they stood behind the counter watching the remaining customers.

'What do you plan to do with your earnings, if you don't mind me asking? New clothes?' Kate asked.

Kim shrugged.

'I enjoy having new outfits from time to time, but I don't follow the newest and craziest trends. I'm thinking about buying a new laptop when I've saved enough. The one I have at the moment is OK, but it works at a snail's pace in comparison to the new ones.'

'Sounds like a good idea. We only had a handful of computers in our school, and not many had a computer at home, either. Nick was always mad about computers, and he pestered my parents until they bought him one. It's all different these days. Everyone has a computer or a smartphone or a tablet.'

'Yeah, the world wouldn't function without computers now. Ryan has an unbelievable digital guiding system on his boat. It's amazing. I keep telling him the only thing it doesn't seem able to do is cook.'

Kate chuckled.

'It sounds daunting. Didn't sailors calculate their positions with a slide ruler and sextant in earlier times? I think sailing round the world solo must be a tremendous challenge, even if they have things like automatic steering. Has Ryan ever done any really long trips?'

'According to Mum he's sailed the Mediterranean, and went right along the Scottish coast last year when it was very stormy. Ryan dreams of a circumnavigation. He has a bookshelf full of books by people who've done it.'

Too curious not to ask, Kate continued.

'Has he a steady girlfriend?'

'No-one special as far as I know, but he's not likely to tell me much about his girlfriends, is he? Since I arrived, he's taken girls out on trips from time to time. They usually came back looking very green about the gills.

'Ryan's girlfriends never seem to last long. My mum goes on at him about it sometimes. What about you, do you have someone special? Have you met the man of your dreams?' Kim's eyes were round like saucers and bright with merriment. 'I think love is a load of old codswallop! There are seven billion people on this earth, why should any two believe that they were meant for each other?'

Kate shrugged.

'It does seem far-fetched, doesn't it? Nevertheless, there are an awful lot of people who say they've found the love of a lifetime. I haven't so far, and in a small seaside town like this, and my working hours, the chances are shrinking. But I don't mind.'

'You could beguile your charming landlord, or perhaps Daniel Craig will walk in here one day for a coffee and it will be love at first sight!'

'He's already taken. Do you fancy Daniel Craig?'

Her hands on her hips, Kim rolled her eyes heavenward.

'Kate! He is ancient, but he'd be fine for you. He has beautiful blue eyes.'

Kate chuckled.

'Get on with you!' She looked at a customer sitting at a window table. She gestured in their direction.

'Look, she's ready to leave. She had a

cappuccino and a lemon tartlet.'

Kim grabbed her pencil and pad and went across. The woman paid, bustled towards the door and left.

* * *

Kate loved the feeling that she only had a staircase journey to her new home.

Looking out of the window, she decided to go for a walk along the beach. It would be dark soon, then she would start unpacking more boxes. Grabbing her jacket and her keys, she skipped downstairs again.

Outside she relished the smell and the sound of the sea. Going down the steps to the sand, she noticed most of the visitors had left for the day. She walked in the direction of the headland.

The sea winds wrestled with her hair and brought colour to her cheeks as she walked along the firm part of the sand where the tide had receded.

Up above, seabirds did their last circles of the day, and she soon found she was a short distance beyond the old pier.

When she reached the huddle of rocks beneath the steep cliffs, she decided reluctantly that she had better turn back. She didn't know the times of the tide, and it would be silly to take a risk. She could do this every day if she wanted to from now on.

By the time she returned home, daylight was fading. She spent the rest of the evening emptying boxes of books into her bookcases along one wall. She stood back and admired the splash of colour they made.

Making a Date

Kate started going for a walk along the beach every day when she closed the café. It cleared her head and helped redirect her thoughts.

One afternoon, when she climbed the steps from the beach, she almost bumped into Ryan. He was still in his business suit but clutching a bulging plastic bag.

He smiled at her and Kate didn't understand why it had such an immediate effect on her composure. She hadn't seen him for several days, but she'd thought of him often.

He looked pleased to see her.

'Hello. Been for a walk?'

Returning his smile, she brushed the hair off her face as he fell into step with her.

'Yes, I go for a walk every day now when I close the café. It helps to split my working day from the rest.'

His expression was full of humour.

'I know what you mean. Settling in?'

'Yes, things are beginning to sort themselves out at last. I intend to invite all of you who helped around one evening soon for drinks. I hope you'll have time to come.' Her colour heightened as she considered his face.

'Gladly.' He paused. 'Actually, I was wondering if you'd like to come on a trip on my boat one afternoon. It's just as relaxing as a walk along the beach. The days are drawing out and there's time for an hour or two's sailing now before daylight fades.'

The invitation was completely unexpected and she hesitated for a moment before answering.

'I'd like that. As long as you realise I could get seasick.'

He looked puzzled.

'Why should you? Not everyone does. Whatever made you think of that?'

Kate hoped Kim wouldn't bite her head off.

'Just something Kim let slip one day

— she confided that your girlfriends came back the worst for wear.'

He threw back his head and laughed.

'She's the limit! I promise you that I never set out with that intention. There's only one way to find out . . . ' He was silent for a second or two and studied her.

'Well, would you like to come, or not?' he asked with dry amusement in his voice.

She bit her lip and nodded.

'Yes, I would. Are you sure you want to go sailing after a day in the office?'

He nodded and looked pleased.

'When I go sailing it's like you taking a walk along the beach. Admittedly, I don't often have time in the week, but you never have a day off, so we have to choose a weekday.' He paused. 'You ought to seriously think about having at least one day off every week. You can't go on working seven days a week for ever.'

She tossed her head.

'I know that. Once I'm established

I'll close all day Monday. The weekends bring in the most profit, and Mondays are generally very slow.'

'Good! I'm glad you've thought about it. What day suits for our trip?'

'You choose.'

He smiled.

'Right! What about next Wednesday?'

Feeling happy and warm inside, she smiled.

'Great.'

'If it's rotten weather, we'll have to choose another date.' He looked down at his plastic bag. 'Kim has invited a friend for a meal and she told me we have nothing suitable so I volunteered to bring something with me on the way home.'

'What have you bought?'

He grinned.

'Some pizza, hamburgers, and various add-ons. We'll only need to throw the rest of the bits and pieces on top of the pizza, and plonk some lettuce and stuff on top of the hamburgers and that's it.'

Her eyes sparkled.

'They'll be happy with either, I'm sure.'

He nodded.

'I'd better get on. I'll phone to confirm our trip and I'll pick you up. My boat isn't moored far from here, but it's in the next cove, so it's too far to walk.'

She nodded and watched as his tall figure turned and strolled off in the direction of the pier. He turned once and waved when he saw she was still there.

* * *

Kate felt elated and looked forward to their trip. She was honest enough to admit that it had something to do with being alone with Ryan.

On Wednesday morning, he rang to confirm their trip.

'Do I need special clothing?' Kate asked.

'Comfortable trousers, a sweatshirt and a waterproof light jacket if you have one. If you intend to remain in one place, bare feet are OK — although that'll be pretty cold at this time of year. Trainers are better to move around because the deck can be slippery and there's deck equipment everywhere on a small boat. I don't want you falling and hurting yourself.'

She felt excitement at the prospect of spending the evening with Ryan.

She closed the café punctually, even hurrying the last customers out so that she had time to go upstairs and change.

The weather was still good. There were only a few wispy clouds in sight, although the sky was predominantly grey. They wouldn't have time for a long trip before darkness, but as it was her first trip, she didn't mind.

Ryan had finished on time, too, because she had just tied her shoes when the bell rang. Grabbing her keys, she hurried downstairs and opened the door.

'You're ready; that's good.' He was wearing jeans and a navy sweatshirt.

Kate was acutely conscious of his tall, athletic physique. He gestured. 'Shall we?'

Kate nodded. She locked the door and they headed for his car which was parked nearby. They followed a coastal road. There was sparse undergrowth on the bordering ground, and the asphalt way twisted and turned.

A few minutes later, he turned off the main road and drove down a narrow track to a small harbour. Boats were bobbing on the water alongside the jetty. He got out and she followed him until he stopped in front of a sleek boat with a single mast.

'This is Aphrodite.'

Aphrodite looked in tip-top condition. It had graceful lines and a shiny hull. To Kate it looked elegant and well designed.

Ryan skipped aboard easily from the jetty and held out his hand.

'Come with me. I'll show you around so you know where everything is.'

Kate skipped aboard and followed

him along a narrow strip of beautifully varnished planks. Her first reaction was that the boat seemed to move constantly, even though they were still in port. The boat was so compact that if she needed to hang on, there were railings within reach everywhere.

'I presume this is what one calls a yacht?' she asked.

He led the way along a narrow side strip to a covered area with the steering equipment and an opening leading down some steps into the cabin. There was a half-circular bench behind the wheel.

'Watch your step and your head! Yes, generally any boat longer than forty feet qualifies as a yacht. The bigger and more expensive it is, the easier it is to define it as a yacht.'

'How long is this one?' She followed him down the wooden steps into a compact, comfortable-looking cabin.'

'Roughly forty feet. The interior also plays a factor, although it's less important to a sailor than the crucial topside impression. It was love at first sight.'

Kate laughed softly.

'Men and cars — what about men and boats?'

'Yes, I think it's the same sentiment!'

The cabin was trim with a small galley, a sitting area, and various storage cupboards wherever space allowed. The fittings were rich wood and highly varnished. She ran her hand over the surface.

Two trim doors were set into the walls. One opened into a bedroom with two comfortable beds with little space in between, and their ends meeting at the bottom where they followed the shape of the V form hull. The other door led to a toilet and shower.

Kate smiled.

'It's all very well organised and compact, isn't it?'

He nodded.

'Right, now you know your way around the boat, let's get moving. Always be careful when you move around. The boom, sails, rigging and anything else isn't static. Could you manage to loosen the mooring lines, and jump back on board again? It would be a great help. I need to steer us out of our berth and into open water.'

'I can swim, so I'll try!' She hoped she wouldn't make a fool of herself.

A few minutes later, they were on their way. She sat on the bench behind the wheel and watched as he took control of the steering wheel and manoeuvred them out into open water.

Plain Sailing?

Ryan glanced at her briefly and smiled. Kate felt her pulse increase. Why did he make her react like this?

'I've checked the weather and we'll just sail round some calm, uncrowded waters so that you get a feel for what it's like.'

Kate leaned back and relaxed to feel the wind on her face. She'd pinned her hair back, but it was now flying all over her face.

'A yacht is not like an alien ship in outer space,' Ryan explained as he continued to steer. 'It is one of the safest, most relaxing and pleasurable means of transportation in the world.'

'You've sailed for a long time?' Kate asked.

'Yes, from as soon as I was old enough and responsible enough. When I was growing up it was my safety valve.

My father was a bank manager. He always expected top marks. Good was not good enough. My uncle saved my sanity by introducing me to sailing. My professional attitude was formed by my father, and my wish for adventure by my uncle.'

'Do you need adventure?'

'Doesn't everyone? We all define adventure differently.'

'Where have you been with this boat?' she asked, brushing her hair out of her face.

'Along the Mediterranean coastline, the Canary Islands, Scandinavia. Last year I went along the west coast of Scotland. That was terrific: beautiful scenery and weather conditions that changed constantly.'

'And you'd like to sail around the world?' Kate noticed they had left the sheltered cove, and the boat was riding the waves. It seemed to be leaning on one side, and the sails were making full use of the wind. They were moving fast, and speeding up even more. It was exhilarating.

He laughed softly.

'Every sailor wants to do that. Perhaps, one day . . . if I'm lucky. I'd like time to linger and enjoy other places and cultures along the way. There is no way I'd just drop everything for a couple of years. I wouldn't enjoy a wonderful time knowing I was returning to a jeopardised future. That's why I bought my house, and why I'm trying to invest in other things. To secure the financial side of things if I ever do set off.'

Kate listened and was surprised, but thinking about it, she realised it was typical of the kind of man he was.

'What kind of other things?'

He moved forward to adjust the boom towards the wind and secured it quickly. Kate admired his proficiency and the muscles rippling under his sweatshirt. He returned to the wheel that he'd fixed during his absence, released it, and took command again. He looked back at her and picked up the conversation.

'I'm already in partnership with a

friend who has a repair and boat-building company. I'm also planning to invest in a small hotel on Dartmoor. I know a couple who intend to convert a sprawling old farmhouse into a family hotel. It won't be a grand, expensive place. They aim for comfortable family and hiker holidays. We haven't sorted out the details yet, but I like the idea and they're nice people. I think it will work.'

'Wow! Most people are happy when they cope with one project. You sound as if you're splitting your life into multiple subdivisions just to make more money.'

'Do I? I'm a silent partner in the firms. I don't interfere in the way they're run.' He shrugged. 'I keep an eye on the book-keeping because I don't intend to see my money disappear, but I don't anticipate that ever happening. I'm just hoping they'll provide me with a nest-egg whenever and if ever I decide to set off.

'Are you so different?' he asked. 'You

could have stayed in your job, but you told me you'd always wanted to have a café and you dropped everything to follow your dream.'

'Perhaps, but I only have the café. I don't intend looking for another object for financial investment.'

'Because you are doing what you always wanted to do. I'm not likely to find a sponsor, so I'll need plenty of cash reserves to do what I want to do. That's the difference between us.'

Trying to sound as casual as she could, she turned to him.

'What about a wife and a family? Do they fit into these plans?'

He shrugged.

'Does getting married and having a family fit into yours? I'll face that situation if or when it happens. I love the feeling of independence I get from sailing and I'd miss it if I had to give it up. I love the feeling that I can decide where to go, when to go, and how long I want to stay there once I've arrived.'

As Kate looked around at the empty

sea, she began to understand, even though she had a minimum of awareness of what normally happened aboard a yacht.

The fact that the wind was carrying them and the man at the wheel was in control of their route was a magical harmony of human nature and the sea. It was a brand-new experience. Time didn't seem to matter and it was a complete contrast to everyday life.

'Are you warm enough? What about seasickness?'

Kate shook her head.

'I'm fine. At this moment I don't feel queasy, either.'

'Good, but don't be afraid to say so, then I'll hightail it for port again. You can't call yourself a real seaman until you've experienced seasickness at least once. Famous sailors have all suffered. There are various traditional remedies: salted anchovy, lemon juice, fixing your sight on the horizon, and some people swear by taking a Vitamin C pill every morning.'

His cap was trying to keep control of

his windblown hair and Kate studied the powerful set of his shoulders in the navy sweatshirt. When he glanced at her briefly, her smile was eager and alive with delight.

Ryan was glad that she was enjoying their excursion. He didn't understand why it was important, but somehow it was. He wanted her to understand the passion he felt for the sea.

'What about a cup of coffee?'

'And what about the steering?'

'I'll set it to automatic.' He glanced around. 'There isn't another boat in sight, and it's not likely that anyone else will be taking a trip now. It will warn me if anyone comes within distance.'

'That's all automatic?'

'It's all down to radar and GPS. Anyone who sails for any length of time needs to sleep sometime, and you need automatic steering. This one is quite sophisticated. It not only keeps the ship on course, it keeps checking the surrounding area and gives a warning down in the cabin if any other boats are in the direct vicinity.'

She nodded.

'Very sophisticated.'

He fixed the wheel then preceded her down into the cabin. In the calm, he gestured to a cushioned bench and set about heating the kettle on the gas stove.

'Tea or coffee?'

'Would it be wrong to ask for tea?' she asked in a friendly, bantering manner. 'In all the films I've seen about yachts, the people only drink coffee.'

'Really?' He smiled and his teeth flashed in his tanned face. 'I've never noticed. You must be very observant. Of course you can have tea if you prefer.'

He found some teabags and two striped mugs.

Kate looked around.

'I like your boat. It's very compact and it looks like you keep everything very tidy. There isn't a lot of space, is there?'

'No fresh milk, I'm afraid. There are some milk sachets if you like.'

She shook her head, accepted her mug from his outstretched hand, and took a sip.

Standing with his hand in one pocket and his mug in the other, he nodded.

'You have to be shipshape. Not just because there isn't much space. Disorder is always a hazard.'

'Where do you keep everything? If you go on a long voyage you need food supplies, clothes and all the rest.'

He laughed softly.

'There's a decent amount of storage room under the bunk beds and I cram as much as I possibly can into the cupboards. Dried food is best, like pasta, or tinned stuff. I keep clothes to the minimum. There's not much call for a tuxedo on board this yacht.' His smile flashed briefly.

'Basic weatherproof clothes and some underwear, that's it! Unless you cross an ocean, you usually follow coastlines and sail into port as often as you can. Once there, you can top up on supplies or go out to eat. This galley is pretty basic. Cooking anything is a challenge, but I manage.'

She looked down at the planking and suppressed a smile. She was imagining him busy at the two-hob cooker. When she looked, he was staring at her.

Kate felt suddenly very self-conscious as Ryan came closer. She automatically stepped back and thought she heard his intake of breath. He immediately turned and busied himself with putting the kettle away. When he twisted back again, his expression was bland and he gestured towards the steps.

'Bring your tea; you can finish it on deck.' He glanced out of one of the small portholes. 'The light is fading and we'd better head for port again.'

Kate didn't know why but she felt disappointed, even though she'd tried to show him she didn't want another meaningless affair. He seemed attracted to her, and she had to keep her distance, otherwise she'd easily find herself tumbling down a slippery slope.

He'd just told her about his dream of

circumnavigating the world. Someone with those kinds of dreams might want relationships, but not serious ones. He didn't include a wife and a family in his plans.

She followed him and settled down again. He was busy so there was no chance for conversation. Kate cradled her mug and looked out across the dull grey waves tossing and turning around them. She could tell he was a good, experienced sailor and she was pleased that she hadn't been seasick. She wondered if he hoped this trip would turn an ordinary friendship into something more.

Perhaps some instinct warned that, given the chance, he was someone who would alter her untroubled lifestyle and she needed to keep him at arm's length. He was interesting, intelligent, and hardworking. He looked good, too. He was danger with a capital D because such feelings would lead her nowhere.

She'd believed Simon was special, and he'd let her down. When she compared the two of them, Simon hadn't been half as interesting or physically attractive as Ryan. Ryan did his own thing.

Unfortunately that meant he had no place for a serious relationship in his plans.

A Heavy Heart

There wasn't much point in trying to hold a normal conversation on the trip back to the jetty. The sound of the sea slapping at the side of the boat and the movement of the wind playing and nudging the sails created a faint humming sound in her ears.

Kate sat facing the wind, enjoying it. She didn't have a clue about the technicalities, but there was somehow a magical harmony between nature and the sea. The waves lulled her and she gave in to her surroundings and just relaxed.

When Ryan had manoeuvred the boat alongside the jetty, he left the wheel long enough to secure the mooring lines. Kate waited for him on board until he'd locked the cabin. He leapt on to the jetty and held out his hand to steady her.

His hold lasted a moment too long, and she had to stop herself snatching her hand away. She told herself not to be silly. Ryan wouldn't force his attentions on any woman. On the contrary, the majority of women would grab any chance to be with him, whatever the future held.

He raised his brows.

'So, back on solid ground again. What's your verdict?'

Her smile was genuine.

'I really enjoyed it. Perhaps it was because I didn't need to do any of the work.'

A grin overtook his features.

'I wouldn't be a good sailor if I asked a non-professional to do anything on their first trip in a small boat. Perhaps next time I'll set you to work.'

She tilted her head to the side.

'Don't tell me I'll have to learn all the different kind of knots before you invite me again,' she quipped.

His mouth quirked.

'That would be a wonderful start.'

He looked at his watch. 'Would you like to go somewhere for a meal, or would you prefer to go home?'

She swallowed hard.

'Home, if you don't mind. I still have countless things to unpack. I'm looking forward to when it's all finished.'

He stuck his thumbs in his pockets and nodded. The lighting on the quay was minimal. Kate couldn't tell if he was disappointed with her answer or not.

'And I'd better check what Kim is doing.' He started to walk to his car.

The car park was empty, and two lampposts offered meagre illumination.

On the journey home, Kate searched for something positive to say, but then she sensed he was busy with his own thoughts, so she remained quiet.

She leaned back into the leather seat and stared out of the side window. There wasn't much to see and Kate was glad the radio was playing soft music to cover the silence.

* * *

Ryan realised Kate's need for emotional commitment had tied her up in knots. She was still afraid she'd get hurt again. His previous girlfriends had been fun, good-time girls, and frivolous. That had suited him at the time because he wasn't looking for commitment.

They were no comparison to the kind of feelings Kate evoked. Her utter determination and commitment to whatever she did were qualities he admired immensely. He wasn't sure how far he wanted to go, he only knew he wanted to know her better and Kate was doing her best to exclude him from any emotional ties. It would be good to gain her trust.

He stopped just around the corner from the shop. He insisted in accompanying her to the door to make sure she was safe. The esplanade was empty and full of shadows.

* * *

When they reached her doorway, Kate was thinking of a way to say goodnight and make amends for her reluctance to agree to emotional involvement, without making it too personal. She suddenly remembered there was something she had intended to say to him anyway.

'I'm asking all the people who helped me with the flat around for drinks and snacks next Friday evening. Do you have time to come? You know most of the others.'

He gave her a nod of consent.

'Thanks. What time?'

'About eight? That gives everyone time to get home from work and relax before they come.'

'Right! I'll see you then.' He tipped his finger to his forehead then leaned forward to kiss her briefly on her cheek.

Kate was glad of the shadows. He couldn't see how her cheeks coloured.

'Thanks for the trip today,' she declared, recovering quickly. 'I really enjoyed it, and I'm delighted that I wasn't seasick. In fact, I'm quite proud of that.'

His smile flashed in the darkness.

'Perhaps you're a born sailor. I'll see

you on Friday then.'

She turned away hastily and fitted her key into the lock. She was glad to be inside in the darkness and leaned against the door for a second, until her hands finally searched for the light switch.

* * *

On Friday evening, Kate felt quite proud as she glanced around her neat living-room. The settees were inviting, the side tables positioned in suitable places, and there were other armchairs and stools in corners for people who didn't want to stand around indefinitely. Her yellow and terracotta colour scheme looked good, although she doubted if many people would notice.

The room was small, and with everyone who'd helped coming, it would be full to bursting. She'd dimmed the lighting, and the old-fashioned sideboard was full of glasses and bottles. Wine and lager occupied most of the room in her fridge, and plates of nibbles, appetisers, and hors d'oeuvres filled the working surfaces in the kitchen.

She hoped she had enough of everything. She changed into clean blue jeans, a white T-shirt and jazzed it up with a pale silk scarf.

Her friend Polly was the first to arrive. She pecked Kate's cheek before she went to throw her jacket on Kate's bed. Polly was tall and slim with shoulder-length ash-blonde hair.

She made nearly all her own clothes and she'd volunteered to make Kate some new covers for her settees. This evening she wore black figure-hugging trousers, a black top displaying an abstract sequin design, dangling earrings, and she carried a huge zebra bag.

Polly ran her hand over the settee cover.

'It looks great,' she remarked. 'That rust colour is just right and that material is stain-resistant, too.'

Kate's eyes twinkled.

'I hope you are not expecting that it will get covered in stains this evening.

My guests are all level-headed and sensible.'

Polly waved her red-tipped fingers.

'You haven't been to as many parties as I have. People tend to forget themselves. That material won't give you any trouble. Apart from red wine. Red wine can be a problem. Someone told me the easiest solution is to douse the spot with white wine, then dab it off.'

Kate laughed and clapped her hands over her ears.

'Polly! Please don't spoil my evening by talking about red wine stains everywhere.'

Polly moved towards the sideboard.

'Oh, good! You've vodka and lime. Just what the doctor ordered!'

Kate laughed softly.

'I doubt if a doctor would recommend vodka. I hope you're not driving home. Anyway, how are things generally?'

Polly mixed her drink, took a gulp, and sighed with satisfaction.

'If someone doesn't give me a lift, I'll get a taxi. Why do I get the feeling that what you're really asking is how Simon is getting on? Badly, I imagine.' She took another sip. 'His new girlfriend expects him to fulfil her every wish and she has expensive tastes. Still, that's his problem. I'm glad you broke up. You didn't suit.'

'I agree, but I didn't realise it at the time.'

'Simon is a phoney and always was. More appearance than reality.'

The doorbell rang. Kate waited as Nick, Monica and Ryan's voices, mixed with those of the neighbours from her previous flat, floated up to her.

Kate was surprised how easily she could pick Ryan's voice out from among all the others. She welcomed them with a smile. Nick and Monica hugged her.

Monica handed her another plate of hors d'oeuvres and her neighbours had brought a bottle of wine. They moved on, leaving her to face Ryan. Her pulse fluttered as he offered her a sudden arresting smile, a huge bunch of flowers, and another bottle of wine.

'Thanks for the invite.' His brown eyes looked almost black in the shadows.

She took the gifts and admired the flowers.

'They're lovely, thank you.'

'You're welcome.' He smiled and went to hang up his jacket in the hallway.

Polly sidled over.

'Kate, who is that?' she whispered. 'He's gorgeous.'

'His name is Ryan Scott,' Kate told her, feeling flustered. 'He's the uncle of a teenager who helps me in the café. He helped me with painting and with moving here.' She paused and added. 'He is also a former boss of mine. He's divisional manager of the company, and probably destined to be a director one day.'

Polly looked at her closely.

'You've never mentioned him before.'

'Because I never had much to do with him. We rarely met at work, and it was mere chance that we met again, and only then because his niece helps me at the weekends.'

Polly prodded her with her elbow.

'And you're keen on him?'

Kate swallowed hard.

'Me? No, what makes you think that? He's not my type. He just happened to help me once or twice.'

'Is he single?'

Kate felt the blood begin to pound in her temples.

'As far as I know. I think he's the free-and-easy type. Someone who doesn't want to be tied down.'

Nick and Monica returned and helped themselves to drinks.

Kate left for a short while to find a vase for the flowers. On her return, she met Ryan's glance. He started to cross the room towards her.

Polly materialised at her side.

'As long as you're sure I'm not barging in on your territory, this may be my lucky night.'

With a twinge of disappointment, Kate straightened her shoulders.

'Carry on. I have no claims on Ryan.'

Polly nodded and moved away

towards Ryan. She struck up a conversation with him and he was too polite not to give her the attention she wanted.

Kate picked up Monica's plate of hors d'oeuvres and placed it amongst all the rest. She rested her hands on the sink for a moment and looked out of the window into the darkness. The doorbell brought her back to earth and she hurried to greet her other guests.

The room was soon buzzing with conversation and laughter. Kate didn't even need to serve anyone. It was soon clear that everyone felt relaxed and happy and knew where to help themselves to drinks and food.

Kate gave up worrying about whether she had enough of everything. The atmosphere was hassle-free and it helped her to enjoy the evening. Most of them knew one another anyway.

Her neighbours from the next-door shop soon relaxed and joined in and Duncan arrived with another big bunch of flowers and a box of chocolates.

Polly had no inhibitions and soon made herself known to anyone who didn't know her. She stuck with Ryan for the rest of the evening, looking up animatedly at him and took every chance to catch his complete attention. Her earrings caught the lamplight as she tossed her head and Kate was too aware of their laughter.

Ryan seemed to enjoy her company. He didn't move away, but he also chatted to anyone standing nearby. Polly's eyes were sparkling brightly and Kate assumed, quite rightly, that she was impressed. Kate marvelled at how hard Polly was trying to win him over.

Kate moved around talking to everyone, but avoided joining Polly and Ryan. They didn't seem to notice. Kate found that ignoring them grew harder as the evening continued. She couldn't help feeling irritated, although she reminded herself that she'd rejected the idea of wanting him herself. She shouldn't feel annoyed if Polly was after him.

Sometimes their glances crossed. Then the way his mouth curled up at the corner and the look in his eyes made her wonder if he was reacting to something Polly was saying, or if he was sending her a message.

She held his glance and found herself starting to blush. She'd made it clear that she wanted to avoid a shallow relationship. Her present thoughts about him were beyond confusing.

She was jealous of her friend and had butterflies in her stomach. She was being very stupid because she and Ryan had different aims in life and she wasn't going to change her mind about that.

Otherwise, the whole evening went well. The food was good, and music from the Eighties and Nineties played in the background. There was plenty to eat and drink and everyone was in high spirits.

Conversations digressed between serious and less sober topics. Duncan could entertain a theatre on his own with his stories.

Kate relaxed, tried to forget about

Polly and Ryan standing together, and just tried to enjoy the evening.

Most of the guests had tomorrow free, but not everyone. It was past one o'clock when Ken from the shop next door announced it was time for them to leave and get some sleep before they had to open their shop the following morning. That reminded others of Kate's café and they began to talk of leaving.

Monica had come by car and she told Kate she'd really enjoyed the evening. She looked as though she meant it. Her eyes sparkled and her colour was high. She hadn't drunk any alcohol all evening and she offered Nick and Duncan a lift home, even though they declared they'd planned on sleeping on Kate's living-room settees.

Kate expected Polly to phone for a taxi, but her heart plunged in frustration when Ryan offered to give her a lift. Kate noticed that Ryan had played with one glass of wine most of the evening and then moved on to non-alcoholic drinks. Kate couldn't guess if Polly was so lively because she was Polly, if she was so animated because of Ryan, or if she'd had one drink too many. She was always bubbly and vivacious.

Kate bit her lip. Polly and Ryan were the last to leave. Polly went to get her coat and pay a quick visit to the bathroom. Ryan came back with his coat, jangled his car keys, and leaned against the doorframe as he watched Kate clearing the plates.

As their gaze met, her heart turned over. He leaned forward and pushed the curls back from her ears. He brushed a gentle kiss across her forehead and then touched her lips with his. It sent a shock wave through her entire system.

She looked up at him, disorientated.

'I've been longing to do that all evening,' he murmured softly.

Fed up with her own frustrations, she frowned.

'It didn't look like that to me.'

His brows lifted and there was a sensuous flame in his eyes. He gave her an irresistible grin.

Polly came into the living-room.

'Ryan, I'm ready to go.'

Kate was confused and knew Polly hadn't seen him kissing her. Was he double-dealing and being deceitful?

He spun around and, crossing to Polly, he shoved a hand under her elbow and propelled her towards the door. Kate followed them in a state of bewilderment. At the door, Polly pecked her cheek.

Ryan met her eyes boldly.

'Thanks for a great evening,' he said.

She listened to the sound of their feet as they went downstairs and then the front door slamming. She skipped down after them and double-locked it before climbing back upstairs with a heavy heart.

He had always confused her, and she'd tried to avoid him. She told herself she was merely physically attracted to someone who was more exciting and persuasive than anyone she'd ever met before, and that included her ex, Simon.

Feeling irritable and restless, she frowned, tidied up the living-room, and washed all the glasses before she got ready for bed.

She couldn't sleep. A vision of him floated into her mind and, although she tried to banish it, she simply couldn't dismiss it for very long. There was no point in agonising over him and wondering if he had underlying motives. She had nothing special that might interest him. Perhaps he was merely a man in pursuit and she was a woman who didn't fall in line easily.

She admitted she was a little jealous, but she definitely wasn't in love.

Frightening Warning

Next morning, despite her late night, Kate opened the café on time. The fog which had been drifting earlier along the esplanade had lifted and the sea was calm and clear.

Kate tightened her apron and switched on the coffee machine. One or two early visitors came in for a cup of coffee and Ken popped in to thank Kate for inviting him and Lottie to the party.

'We enjoyed ourselves last night, love. Nice people and good food.'

Kate smiled.

'I'm glad. Yes, they are all nice, and that includes you and Lottie. It's good to know you're next door in an emergency.'

Kim arrived on time and from then on they were very busy. After lunch, there was a short lull and they had a chance to speak.

'Your party seems to have gone well,' Kim commented. 'Ryan didn't get home until after three. I heard him come in.'

Kate answered with a bland smile. He and Polly had left just after one o'clock and Polly lived less than 20 minutes away. She swallowed the ache in her throat.

'Yes, I enjoyed it, too.'

Kate was relieved to see a new customer arrive. Kim saw her, too.

'I'll get it. Finish your coffee. The table by the door wants to pay, too.'

Kate watched her deal competently with the customers. It gave her time to absorb the information she'd just received. It made her more determined to concentrate on her café and her work.

* * *

That evening Polly rang.

'Hi, Kate. Thanks for last night. It was super. I wouldn't have met Ryan otherwise. He's such an interesting man, and did you know he actually owns a yacht?'

Kate paused for a moment to collect her thoughts.

'Yes, I know.' She decided not to mention she'd already been on a trip. 'Apparently Ryan loves sailing.'

'I gave him my telephone number,' Polly continued, 'and I'm hoping he'll invite me out one day. That would be great. He's different to most of the men I've met. He's polished, polite — and he's certainly not bad looking either!'

It sounded like the modern woman with flawless make-up, pampered skin, and magical sewing skills was also a woman who was looking for a partner. Kate always believed Polly was the party queen among party queens. She took a deep breath.

'Yes, I suppose you're right. We must get together soon for a chat. Are you going out tonight?'

'A friend invited me to go to a disco in town. I can sleep late tomorrow so I may as well. I hoped to hear from Ryan, but he probably likes to keep women guessing. There's no point in hanging around at home waiting, is there?'

'No, I suppose not. I'm going for a walk before the daylight fades then I'm going to vacuum the flat. I'm having an early night with a book.'

'Yuk! You'll have to organise things better. Otherwise you'll never meet anyone worthwhile. You need to have free weekends. That's when all the action happens.'

'Polly, I was glad to get away from the hectic routine of going out and partying every weekend. I'm doing what I've always wanted to do.'

'But you'll never meet anyone in that place. You'll end up known as the sweet little old lady with a teashop on the seafront!'

Kate laughed.

'I don't mind. Perhaps I'll be able to afford reliable help at the weekends one day. If I do, I will have a weekend off now and then. I already think I can close on Mondays because business is very slack. Having Monday off will give me time to fit in other things I have to do.'

'Like what?'

'Oh, sorting out any administrative stuff, going to the bank, to the doctor or the dentist.'

'You're not ill, are you, or losing your teeth already?' Polly's voice heightened.

Kate chuckled.

'No, of course not.' She didn't think that being lovesick qualified as an illness. 'I'll give you a call one evening next week. Enjoy the disco.'

'I will. Bye, Kate!'

* * *

Kate lay in bed, unable to ignore the truth any longer. They didn't match, but that hadn't stopped her falling in love with Ryan Scott. Her heart was hammering and her mind raced and circled as she finally acknowledged reality.

Next morning she was glad to think

about her café, and hurried to get ready. She hoped for another busy day. Grabbing her keys, she went downstairs and opened the door.

There was a slight breeze laden with the smell of salt coming in from the sea and Kate took a deep breath. Seagulls circled above her and they looked down, disappointed that she had no food for them.

She glanced along the empty seafront and listened to the waves plunging on to the sand down below. Apart from having the complication of Ryan, she was sure she'd done the right thing.

Locking the flat door, she turned to go inside the café and stopped in her tracks.

LEAVE WITCH; GET OUT! The words were smeared in bright red paint across the windows and some of the frame.

A gasp caught in Kate's throat and for a moment she couldn't breathe. She couldn't believe it. Her befuddled brain wondered how she was going to remove the paint before it was time to open up. She touched one letter of the printing gingerly with the tip of her finger. It was hard.

Her mind spun and she still couldn't think logically. Ken and Lottie came towards her and smiled at her until they saw the windows. They checked their own premises, but there was nothing.

Ken whistled and threw his arm round her shoulder.

'Who would do such a thing? Delinquents and vandals, no doubt! We'll call the police.' He realised Kate was shaking. 'Go inside and sit down. I'll phone them.'

Kate nodded and somehow managed to get the key into the lock and went inside. The appearance of the red lettering didn't look any better from inside. The first weak rays of sunshine seemed to accentuate and outline the bright crimson colour.

When she was eyeing it, Kim came along and stopped instantaneously, staring incredulously at the words. When she spotted Kate, she came inside.

She made a face.

'Someone must be sick in their head to do that.' She looked at Kate's face. 'Like a cup of tea?'

Trying to sound normal, Kate nodded. 'Ken is calling the police. They'll probably turn up soon.'

Kim went behind the counter and there was soon a clatter of crockery. Kate sat with her hands tightly locked, still staring at the lettering, and unable to believe what had happened. Kim returned a couple of minutes later with a tray.

'Here you are. My gran maintains strong, sweet tea always helps in an emergency.' She poured a cup of tea and shoved the sugar bowl towards Kate.

Kate added a couple of spoons of sugar and cradled the cup between her hands. She took a sip of the hot liquid. It would take more than a cup of tea to settle her nerves, but it gave her something to do with her hands.

'Would you like me to make you a sandwich?'

Kate shook her head. Two women

approached the café door, but stopped dead when they read the scarlet words written across the windows. They bent their heads and whispered for a few seconds, before they walked on with their eyes focused ahead of them.

Kate indicated towards them, tears building at the back of her eyes.

'Look, they were probably our first customers of the day and now they're frightened off!'

'Oh, don't worry about them. If they had any sense they would realise it is only a wind-up.'

'A prank? A hoax? I don't think so.'

The door burst open and Ryan came in. He hurried over and his eyes oozed sincerity and kindness.

'Hey!' He sat down opposite Kate and pressed her hands between his.

Kate wished she could ask him to hold her tight. To her embarrassment, there were tears threatening and he noticed.

He pulled her to her feet and hugged her tightly.

'I understand why you're upset,' he

muttered, stroking her hair, 'and it's a truly awful thing to happen to anyone, but you need to focus on what's important. The police are just behind me. They'll be here in a minute. They're sure to ask if you can think of anyone who would do such a thing.'

She didn't try to free herself from his grasp, and she didn't even care what Kim thought. She shook her head and met his gaze inches away from her. The tantalising smell of sandalwood and her light flowery perfume mingled and rose between them.

She felt his compassion and it helped more than he realised.

Two men entered. One wore a police officer's uniform, while the other was in civilian clothes.

Kate freed herself and turned to face them.

'Good morning, miss. Are you the manager?' one of the officers asked.

'Good morning. Yes.'

'When did you discover it? Do you have any idea who could have done it?'

Kate's voice steadied and she felt quite rational again.

'I came down to open up just before nine. Someone must have done it during the night. Painting or spraying is a silent occupation, isn't it? I live above the café, but I didn't hear or see anything.'

'And you have no idea who it could be? Do you have a competitor or a personal foe?'

She shook her head defiantly.

'I haven't been here very long. I don't think there's another teashop in the town.' She looked at Ryan and he shook his head. 'This is Ryan Scott; he lives in the town. He's a friend of mine.'

'I'm afraid it's not very likely that we'll find whoever did it,' the officer in civilian clothes warned, although his expression was compassionate. 'Graffiti goes on all the time, although it's rare in this town. I'll get our team in to check for fingerprints and take some photos. I imagine you want to get it removed as soon as possible?'

Kate straightened.

'Yes, of course. Having that splashed across the windows won't do my business any good.'

He nodded understandingly.

'Do you know how I can remove it?' Kate asked.

'If you don't have special insurance, and from experience I'd say few people do, your best bet of getting most of it off would be with one of those hob scrapers. Do you know what I mean?'

Kate nodded.

'I use one on my oven when I have spills.'

'The window frames are more of a problem, but there are special graffiti removers and if you have a word with one of the men at the DIY shop they'll be able to help.'

Ryan retorted.

'I'll handle that. I'll bring a new scraper, some rubber gloves if I need them, and I'll ask about the window frames.' He addressed the policeman. 'Could you be obliging and speed things up? We know it's the weekend, but I'm sure you realise that something like this is very detrimental to business, and we need to get things sorted out as soon as possible.'

He smiled understandingly.

'We'll do our best, sir. We have a camera in the car. We'll take a handful of photos straight away and get on to one of our fingerprint chappies. He lives not far from here and, if we explain, I think he'll help and won't take long.

'If you're going to the DIY store, I wouldn't be surprised if he's finished by the time you get back. In the meantime I'll take down all the details I need from Miss . . . ?'

'Watson, Kate Watson,' Kate supplied.

'And then we hope we have more luck than usual and find the culprit. It's a real shame, but that's how things are these days. In my days, kids pinched apples or knocked on doors and ran away, but today they seem to have fun spoiling other people's possessions.'

Kate suddenly remembered the school gang. Were they behind this? She was tempted to mention it, but she hesitated. She couldn't make accusations like that.

She'd talk to Kim after the police left.

Business as Usual

A few minutes later, Ryan was on his way to the nearest DIY store, and the two policemen were sitting at one of the tables. The uniformed one filled his notebook with the details while enjoying a cup of coffee. He got up and his companion joined him. He held out his hand.

'Thank you, miss. We'll be back in a couple of minutes to take some photos and we'll get on to the fingerprint chap. We'd like you to come down to the station to sign a statement at the beginning of the week. If we make any progress, we'll be in touch and if anything else unusual happens, you just get in touch with me.' He handed her his card. 'The coffee was very good. I'll pop in with my wife one day when we're in the vicinity. She likes a cuppa and a piece of cake when we go out somewhere.'

Kate smiled, feeling slightly better now.

'Do. Thanks, and I hope you find who did it and why.'

He shrugged and the two men left. The café was still empty but Kim had written BUSINESS AS USUAL on several large pieces of cardboard from boxes in the store room. She went outside to attach them to the windows. They covered a lot of the red lettering.

When she came back, Kate gave her a hug and with her eyes glistening again, she smiled.

'Thank you!'

To her surprise, people still came in and also sympathised with her about the vandalism. She and Kim were busy, especially as time went on.

Ryan returned with a scraper and a tin of something he explained was for removing graffiti from wooden framework. They might have to repaint parts of the frames, but Kate still had some paint and no-one would notice the difference.

Luckily, the weather was mild for working outside. Kate told Ryan that she could phone for help from someone in the family but he brushed her suggestion aside and began to scrape gently at the glass.

While serving people in the café, she sometimes looked at him concentrating on the job, and mused that he worked in the same way he did everything, with determination and tenacity. She didn't understand why he gave up so much time to help, but she was too busy to dwell on that at present.

She dragged him inside for a break after a couple of hours. They chatted casually as he drank coffee and polished off a pile of sandwiches.

Kim viewed them speculatively from behind the counter and vowed to watch them more closely in future. Had she missed something important? Ryan was acting very protectively. Kim recalled his horrified reaction when she'd phoned to tell him and she couldn't believe how quickly he'd got down here from the bungalow.

He was always responsive if someone asked for his support or help, but she'd never seen him so agitated before. She'd have to discuss it with her mum next time they talked and ask what she thought about it all.

By early afternoon, Ryan was finished. He fetched a bucket of water with washing-up liquid and gave the window a final wash down. When Kate went outside to look at the result, she was delighted.

Her voice mirrored her pleasure.

'I can't thank you enough, Ryan. You've spent your whole Sunday doing it, although I expect you planned to go sailing or do something else.'

He surveyed his work.

'Yes, it looks shipshape again, although I bet you'll need to clean the windows properly and touch the framework up here and there. That stuff the chap in the DIY recommended was great, and perhaps it helped because the paint was still fresh. It hadn't had time to harden completely.'

He handed her the bucket and

clapped his hands.

'I'll be off. I have to sort out a report for a meeting tomorrow.' He looked up at the sky where clouds were scudding across between patches of blue. 'Tell Kim she can walk home today, but not to loiter on the way.'

'I can drive her home. That's the least I can do after how you've helped me today.'

He shrugged, then nodded.

'Either way, tell her to text me that she's on her way.'

Kate knew he took his responsibility seriously.

'I will.' She felt completely mixed up as they stared at each other for a moment. She hoped for some kind of physical contact, but that wasn't likely to happen with people staring out of the windows and with Kim in the background — and she reminded herself she had always backed away from him in the past.

With his hands thrust into the pockets of his jacket, he gave her a parting nod and strode off down the esplanade in the direction of the cliff path.

'I didn't want to mention it to the police,' Kate muttered to Kim while they were clearing up, 'but do you think that gang had something to do with it?'

Kim stopped stacking the plates.

'Gosh! I hadn't thought of that,' she uttered. 'You're right! I'll corner them tomorrow and see how they react. They may give themselves away.'

Kate already knew they weren't likely to open up to her if she asked them, so she nodded.

'But do be careful! Don't push them. I don't want them getting angry with you. Promise me?'

'Yeah, no problem. They're not so aggressive these days. They leave me alone. I'll ask my friend Janice to come with me when I confront them.'

Kate hoped it was all right to let Kim tackle them. They cleared up, and Kate drove Kim home, dropping her off at the garden gate.

She went back to the café and cleaned the windows. Ryan had done his best, but she soon had them looking even better.

It had been a tiring day, so she was glad to put her feet up and listen to some music before going to bed.

She thought about the way Ryan had held her and her heart fluttered. She revelled in the memory until something at the back of her mind reminded her that, after he and Polly left her party, he hadn't arrived home until very late. Where had he been?

* * *

Kim called in the following afternoon. Most of the tables were empty so she and Kate could chat.

'I asked them, and they denied having anything to do with it. Funnily enough, I believe them. I can't explain why but I noticed that one or two looked very frightened after I mentioned the police were involved and they looked genuinely gobsmacked when I described what had happened.'

'Well, thanks for trying, and don't bother them again. I'm glad that you are beginning to feel happier in the school, I don't want that to change.'

To their amazement, a few minutes later, Roger Makepeace came shuffling through the door and came straight up to the counter.

Kim spoke first.

'What do you want?'

Shoving some hair out of his face and moving restlessly, he addressed Kate.

'She told me what happened. I want you to know it wasn't me, or any of the others.'

'Why should I believe you?'

He shrugged.

'Because it's the truth. I have enough problems in school, and with my old man, He's breathing down my neck about my exam results. I'm not stupid and wouldn't do anything to snowball the present situation.' He nodded in Kim's direction.

'She mentioned that the police are involved, so I wanted to make sure you don't suggest it was anything to do with us.' He looked down at his bright green trainers. When he looked up, his expression was troubled.

Kate believed him.

'I haven't mentioned anything to the police about you, or the others.'

He nodded and, to her surprise, he sounded almost grateful.

'She told us that, too, so I'll be glad if it stays that way.'

Kate wiped the surface of the counter.

'If I find you are lying . . . '

'I'm not. I can't afford any more hassle.'

Kate nodded.

'OK. You're lucky that I'm in a benevolent mood. Why don't you make sure you stay out of trouble permanently?'

With a relieved glance in Kim's direction, he ambled towards the door.

Kate laughed as he exited.

'Who'd have thought he had enough guts to face you personally!' Kim exclaimed.

* * *

When Kim went home, she told Ryan about Roger Makepeace's unexpected visit. He rang Kate. Merely the sound of his voice caused mayhem with her pulse rate.

'Hi, Kate. Kim just told me how that boy turned up at the café to declare he was innocent. He must be pretty scared to go that far.'

Kim managed a laugh.

'Yes, and somehow I believe him.'

'To be honest, so do I. The police didn't sound very hopeful that they'd find who did it, so it will probably get lost in police archives.'

'Who knows? Let's hope for the best. Feeling better now?'

Her laugh was shaky, but she was candid.

'Yes, thanks. I've adjusted. Perhaps it was just a fluke, although why they chose my place I still don't understand. Whoever did it knew the owner was female.'

'We'll have a chat when I get back.'

'You're going away?'

'A week in London. My cleaning lady

is moving in to keep an eye on Kim. I've done it before and it works out fine. Kim doesn't mind.'

Kate nodded.

'Kim can always turn to me for help if she needs it.'

'She knows that. She likes you. I hope my workers think as highly of me as she does of you.'

Kate coloured.

'Have a safe journey and thank you for your help on Sunday. I wish I could repay it. I'll have to think of something suitable.'

His voice was full of amusement.

'I can think of lots of ways you could do that, but we'll talk about that another time.'

There was a click and the connection was broken.

Things That Go Bump in the Night

The knowledge that Ryan was away put a damper on the week. Kate phoned Nick to tell him what had happened.

'Are you OK?' he asked, his voice full of concern.

'I'm fine now. There was no physical danger, just the deplorable mess on the windows. Ryan spent most of Sunday getting it off.'

'Why didn't you call me? I would have helped.'

'I know that. Kim phoned him when she arrived and Ryan came straight away. I suggested getting other help, but he insisted it wasn't necessary.'

'Ryan seems very involved. Is there something going on between you two?'

Kate coloured.

'No, he's just very helpful. When I

worked at the supermarket I assumed he was condescending and stuck-up, but he isn't really.'

'If everything's OK now, I might pop down to see you at the weekend.'

'I look forward to seeing you.'

* * *

Next morning, just as she was about to leave the flat, the phone rang. It was Gerald Hardwick.

'Good morning! I hear someone has been splashing graffiti across the windows.'

'Who told you?'

'I may not live in the town, but I still have connections, and news spreads fast.'

'Well, yes, there was a problem, but it's been resolved. Everything looks as good as new.'

'I hope so, for your sake as well as mine. I'm not insured for that kind of thing.' There was a pause. 'If you ever decide you want to move out, just say the word. I could get a new tenant in no time at all . . . '

'I expect you would, especially now I have modernised and repaired everything. I have no intention of leaving. My contract is for five years and I'm sticking to that.'

'I was only making an offer. Something like this can be upsetting.'

'Thanks for your concern. I have to go and open up the café now, Mr Hardwick.'

'I wish you'd call me Gerald.'

'Bye, Mr Hardwick.'

* * *

Something woke Kate. Drowsily, she fought with consciousness and tried to focus on her bedside clock.

There it was again. A sound of something hitting the window. Was it stormy outside and pebbles or shingle were spraying the window so high up?

She grabbed her dressing gown and made her way to the living-room.

Flooding it with light, she went to the window, but there was nothing unusual to see or hear. She checked the view from other windows with similar results. Perhaps it was her imagination. She went back to bed.

The following night the same thing happened, and Kate knew now that it wasn't her imagination. For the next two nights, she rushed to the window after the sounds got her out of bed where she'd been lying half-awake, waiting expectantly for it to happen.

Had she misjudged the atmosphere in this sleepy seaside town? Firstly, the aggressive kids from the school, then someone spraying graffiti, and now somebody was playing tricks in the middle of the night.

She thought about the detective's card but reasoned they wouldn't station someone to watch outside her flat just because someone was disturbing her sleep.

A day or two passed without incident and she wondered if the culprit was becoming fed up of sneaking around at three o'clock in the morning.

By the weekend, she had almost forgotten it. Then during the early hours of Sunday, the same sound woke her again. She was angry, but also getting nervous because someone was clearly singling her out.

Secretly she wished there was some reason for Ryan to phone her. He was sensible. He wouldn't think she was silly and being hysterical. He didn't phone, but why should he?

The sounds of something tapping against the window went on intermittently, and the following Sunday morning before she opened the café, she noticed there were pebbles on the window-sill.

Even Kim noticed Kate was paler than usual when they were stacking the clean crockery.

'You look like you've had a bad night. Feel ill?'

'No, it's just that I haven't been sleeping very well for a few days. I expect that's it.'

'Problems with the café? Or has Roger been making trouble again?'

Kate laughed.

'No, the café is doing fine, and I don't think Roger will bother me again.' She took a deep breath. 'I'm thinking of closing on Mondays. That will give me a day off.'

Kim picked up a tea cloth and started polishing the spoons.

'That's good. Everyone needs a break now and then. You haven't been open long, but you can't go on working seven days a week.'

'What about you? You're in school all week, and you come in here on Saturday and Sunday. That doesn't leave you much spare time either, does it?'

'Oh, I enjoy coming. It's completely different from school. A couple of the other girls have asked me if there was a chance of them working here, too. If I didn't come, you can be sure there are others ready and waiting.'

'Your job is safe as long as you want

it. Someone came in the other day and asked where you were. It shows how people think you are part of the place already.'

'If I ever want a day off I'll ask one of the others to fill the gap. You're going to need someone when I leave anyway, so it'll give you a chance to test someone else.'

'Are you leaving?' Kate touched her arm. 'This place wouldn't be the same without you.'

Kim breathed on the glass and polished vigorously.

'Oh, I'll be around for a couple of months yet, but my mother mentioned last week that Dad's next posting is likely to be Athens or Bogota.'

Kate whistled softly.

'Wow!'

Kim looked relaxed.

'I don't care where we go. I just like the idea of being with my mum and dad again. Mum seems to miss me. Our chats via Skype aren't enough any more.'

Kate nodded.

'I bet.'

Some customers came in and Kim threw the tea cloth aside and grabbed her pencil and pad.

There wasn't much time for talk after that. A friend from school came to collect Kim when they finished for the day. Kate could see she had made friends at last.

In a way, Kate envied her. She'd grow up to be a cosmopolitan woman who was comfortable wherever she happened to be. She'd already learned you had to accept people as they were, not as you wanted them to be.

After clearing everything ready for next morning, Kate went upstairs and put the kettle on for a cup of tea.

As she was pouring the water into the teapot, the phone rang.

'Hello.' There was no answer. 'Hello?' Kate repeated.

There was a crackle but no reply. Perhaps someone had dialled a wrong number.

She fixed a tray with the rest of the things for her tea, and the phone rang again. The same thing happened.

She checked the last number on the handset — Withheld.

Kate felt uneasy. She immediately wondered if the pebbles against the window and the anonymous phone calls were connected.

She thought about disconnecting the phone, but that would be counterproductive. Friends or family might call and start to worry.

Less than an hour later, the phone rang again and the same thing happened. When it rang a couple of minutes later, she was really jumpy.

'Whoever you are, stop calling unless you have something to say to me,' she snapped.

'Kate? It's me! What's the matter? Is someone annoying you with anonymous calls? Kim told me you didn't look too good. I wanted to ask if I could help.'

Conflicting emotions promptly emerged. She was delighted to hear Ryan's voice, but she didn't want to explain or involve him.

'Oh, nothing too dramatic. Someone keeps calling, and doesn't say anything when I pick up the receiver. It's a bit creepy but nothing significant. Probably just kids larking around.'

His voice sounded agitated.

'How long has it been going on?'

'The telephone calls?' she said, trying to sound unconcerned. 'Only since I closed this evening. It's nothing to worry about. If kids are responsible, they'll soon tire of it, and do something else that's just as stupid.'

'Yes, it could be kids, of course, but I haven't forgotten the graffiti. Put those two things together and it could mean something completely different.'

Kate ignored the memory of sounds on the window — she didn't intend to mention that on top of the other things. She paused too long.

'Look, I'll come around. We need to talk about this.'

'No, Ryan, that's not necessary. I can manage.' It was too late; there was a buzzing noise. He'd cut the connection.

The Magic of His Kiss

Torn between wanting to see him, and knowing that his physical presence was always tricky for her to handle, Kate rushed to brush her hair and renew her lipstick.

As she viewed herself in the mirror, she noted the heightened colour on her cheeks. It was amazing how the mere idea of him sent her senses reeling.

She put the kettle on to make coffee and checked the state of the living-room. In what seemed no time at all, the door-bell rang and she waited for him to climb the stairs. His gaze travelled her face and searched her eyes.

'You shouldn't have bothered. I'm fine, honestly,' she said, hoping she sounded convincing.

His smile was kind and understanding.

'You shouldn't ignore it.' He tossed

his jacket over the back of a convenient chair. 'First there was the mysterious business of the graffiti which was never solved, and now you're getting anonymous phone calls.' He tilted his head to the side. 'You haven't been needling any opponents by any chance, and this is their method of paying you back?'

She shook her head.

'Coffee?'

He nodded and she fetched the waiting tray from the kitchen.

On her return, he was already sitting on the couch.

'I'm the only teashop in the town. As far as I know, I haven't any competitors. I use local suppliers for everything, as much as possible.' She handed him a mug of coffee and he leaned forward to add a spoonful of sugar.

He took a sip and slid his free arm along the back of the settee. When he spoke there was dry amusement in his voice.

'Then we can forget that possibility?'

She licked her lips.

'Yes, I don't understand it. I have never knowingly offended anyone.' Her hidden pleasure at having him near let her sense of humour take over and she laughed.

'Perhaps someone has a voodoo doll of me hidden away in their cupboard and keeps sticking pins in it every time they have a bad day at the office.'

There was teasing laughter in his expression.

'It doesn't sound like you've given anyone reason enough to annoy you that badly.'

She shrugged.

'Who knows?'

He leaned forward and, resting his arms on his thighs, he dropped his hands, cradling the mug between his legs.

'When did these phone calls start?'

'Only a couple of hours ago. I didn't think it was unusual the first two or three times, but then I remembered the pebbles . . . ' She put her hand to her mouth.

He looked up with interest.

'What pebbles?'

She was livid with herself. For a moment, she thought about making something up, but then decided that would be wrong. She haltingly explained about the sounds against the window.

His expression darkened.

'And why didn't you mention that earlier?' He put his mug on the table with a clatter. 'Adding all these things together, there's definitely something wrong here. It isn't OK, so don't pretend that it is. For a start, you should report it to the police.'

She hesitated and her words mirrored her uncertainty.

'The police aren't likely to wrench someone away from doing serious work to sort out childish pranks, are they?'

'No,' he conceded, 'but there's also no point in sticking your head in the sand, either.' He was pensive now and didn't sound so annoyed. 'I'm still trying to figure it out. Who has an advantage if they frighten you?'

She shrugged.

'No-one, as far as I'm aware. The shop was vacant for a long time before I took it on. The other shops near the esplanade deal in completely different things. I haven't pushed anyone out, nor do I present direct competition to anyone else nearby.

'There aren't any shops of any kind on the pier, just that small games arcade at the beginning and a small kiosk selling ice-cream and soft drinks.

'I don't compete with them because if someone wants a soft drink from me, they get it in a glass and drink it here. I checked that sort of thing out before I decided this was the right place for me to come.'

Her mouth twitched.

'I'm not trying to pinch anyone's boyfriend or husband, either, so there should be no jealous adversary anywhere in the vicinity as far as I know.'

Ryan looked exasperated.

'You should take this seriously. There's something funny going on. Did you hear the sounds last night?'

She nodded.

'I tried to ignore it, but it didn't work.' He got up.

'I think it would be a good idea for me to spend the night downstairs in the café.'

Kate's mouth opened.

'What?'

He continued as if she weren't there.

'The windows will give me a good view if someone prowls around in the middle of the night. They'll need to be within throwing distance of your windows.

'You just need to phone me as soon as you hear anything — I'll put my mobile on vibrate — and I'll grab them. They've probably figured out that they have time to disappear before you can dash downstairs and find out who's responsible.'

'You can't spend the night in the café,' Kate objected. 'You'll be tired out tomorrow and it's cold in the night. The heating is automatically turned down.'

'Let that be my problem. I want to

get to the bottom of this, and my plan is as good as any I can think of.'

'What about Kim? You can't leave her alone in the house. She'll worry if she wakes up and no-one is there.'

He grinned.

'As fate has it, she's spending the night with a friend, and they'll be going straight to school from there tomorrow. Any other objections?'

Kate felt flabbergasted, but his steamrollering worked. He noticed and looked satisfied.

'Right, I'll just pop home and get some warm clothes and night-vision binoculars. What time did you normally hear the noises?'

'It's varied, but usually between three and four in the morning.' She paused. 'Look Ryan, are you sure about this? You're not obligated to me to help, you know that. I could always ask my brother or even Duncan to stop overnight and try to find out who's behind it.'

He nodded.

'I know, but I want to help.' There was a lengthy pause as they looked at each other. 'Is Duncan someone special?' Ryan suddenly asked. 'I've wondered that several times when I've seen you together.'

'Duncan? No. He's Nick's best friend, but there is nothing romantic between us.'

His voice sounded lighter.

'But he would like to . . . ?'

Kate brushed the hair from her face.

'You can't always choose where your affections go, can you?'

'True!'

She looked and noticed his lips had an upward turn.

He jumped up. Kate glanced up at him as he stopped very close. She could smell sandalwood and she wondered if he would taste of spearmint toothpaste. She found it almost impossible to meet his gaze. The air had left her lungs.

He stepped even closer and pulled her into his arms. His kiss was testing her and she could tell he was being careful. He probably remembered how she'd shied from any familiarity in the past.

She mused that his kiss felt like a combination of adventure and protection, and Kate didn't want to pull away any more.

He wrapped his arms tighter and his body pressed against hers. His kiss deepened and it was getting progressively more difficult for her to remember why she'd ever wanted to avoid this man. He awakened such magic in her with just one kiss.

His kiss softened and he held her gently at arm's length. He teased with another kiss across her forehead.

When her breath evened again, she eyed him guardedly.

'I don't think that was a good idea.'

'Why not?' His eyes sparkled with laughter.

'Because we want different things from life.' She cleared her throat awkwardly. 'You have plans to travel. You're a sailor with dreams of circumnavigating the world. I'm content to make my life here.'

He immediately realised that she'd

been thinking about the situation. That gave him more hope than she knew.

'My dearest Kate, my plans for making that kind of journey is far in the future. I don't even know if I'll ever manage to pull it off.'

'But you already go on long sailing holidays,' she replied, sounding more resolute than she felt. 'A girlfriend would only cause problems and it would end in constant quarrels. I don't believe in relationships that are stopgaps. It's better not to start something that's doomed to end in disappointment.'

He held her glance.

'Kate, it's true that I've never had what one calls a long-term girlfriend. It always seemed too much of a hassle, and I didn't feel any loss when a girlfriend called it off.

'I know that sounds terrible, but they were girlfriends who were looking for the same kind of relationship I wanted. They wanted to enjoy themselves without obligations. They were interested in my lifestyle because they thought social standing or money was important. I knew that and it suited me fine.

'Your friend Polly is like that. She's nice, but status and money play a big role in her way of thinking. She was simply too animated, too eager, the other day. I was glad to get away and go for a long walk along the cliff before I went home.'

Kate looked down.

'I see.' She looked up. 'I don't pretend to understand your attitude, but it's your life, not mine.'

'That was all before I met you.'

She held her head steady and her breath caught in her lungs.

'And that means I'm different? What's different about me?'

'Everything. It's hard to put it into words. It's how you love your café, your determination, your loyalty to your friends and family, your love of the sea and your humour. It's your whole personality. I have never met anyone before who has this kind of effect on me. You are also beautiful — even when you're wrapped up in your café apron! You have it all.'

Kate could have told him that no-one had told her anything so breathtaking before, but there was a lump in her throat and she couldn't get the words out.

She saw the sincerity in his eyes and knew he wasn't playing her along. She swallowed.

'If I ever met someone I wanted to spend my life with, I'd like a home and a family,' she told him.

'And where's the problem? I'd like that, too.'

'You can't daydream about sailing the seven seas, and still expect to have a family waiting patiently for you,' she replied, trying to sound perfectly rational.

'Let's get this straight. My idea about sailing round the world is a long time in the future, if ever at all. I couldn't afford to do so at present, and I'm not aiming to, either.

'Perhaps, if I'm very lucky, I'll be experienced enough and solvent enough when I'm much older. I also hope that I can include my family in any expeditions in the future. For the time being, I am quite happy cruising home waters.

'If you give us a chance, I hope you'll grow to enjoy sailing as much as I do. My yacht is definitely big enough for two, and I hope my earnings will keep pace with demands if we need something bigger.'

'We?' Her voice broke.

He laughed softly and hugged her tight. His voice was calm and his gaze was steady.

'Of course! I'm talking about us. I never thought it would happen to me, but I'm in love with you, Kate. I fell hook, line and sinker, and if you keep pushing me away, I'm going to end up extremely miserable. Do I have a chance? Do we have a chance?'

She stared at him in astonishment and was speechless. She knew enough about him to realise he was honest and telling the truth. Her heart pounded and a new and unexpected warmth surged through her. The thrill from the knowledge he wanted her absolutely amazed her.

Her face creased into a dazzling smile. She reached up and ran her hand down his face. He turned to one side and kissed it.

'That's all I need to know. We now have all the time we need to sort everything out.'

Kate nodded.

'First of all we have to solve this business of pebbles and phone calls.'

Drawing a deep breath and thinking sensibly again, she pulled herself together.

'OK. I'll make a flask of coffee for you, and some sandwiches.'

His face was eager and alive with affection and delight. He kissed her again.

'I'll go home to get what I need. If I stay much longer I'll find myself thinking about how I can stay here and be with you to watch the dawn breaking, instead of catching who's behind the pebble throwing.' He lifted the palm of her hand to his lips and kissed it again, before he swiftly turned and clattered downstairs.

Kate felt as if she were dreaming, but her burning desire for another kiss told her this time love was for real. With her mind spinning, she went into the kitchen.

When he returned, his kiss left her with shivers of delight.

'I'm so glad that I've found you.'

She kissed him back, savouring every moment.

'Can I come downstairs with you?'

He looked at his watch. It was past midnight.

'And who is going to listen up here and warn me if anything hits the window?'

She shrugged. Now that she'd found him she didn't want to let him go.

'It's important to find out who's behind it. It is only for a couple of hours. I don't intend to ever leave you in any kind of danger; not tonight, not ever.'

Kate gave in and he took her flask and the sandwiches and went to take up his position downstairs.

Time dragged, but she also felt euphoric and her mind was turning cartwheels. As three o'clock approached, she held her phone with Ryan's number ready and waiting.

She didn't wait in vain. The window rattled with the newest round of pebbles shortly after three o'clock. She pressed the button. Downstairs she heard the sound of the café door opening and then scuffling followed by yelping sounds.

She grabbed her coat and ran. She was fearful for Ryan, but when she reached the esplanade the lighting showed he had things under control. He had Gerald Hardwick on the floor, with his knee on his back, and Hardwick's arm twisted in deadlock.

She was shocked.

'Mr Hardwick! You're behind it. Why?'

'I want you out. I need to sell the place. I need money fast.' He wriggled to free himself of Ryan's firm grip.

Ryan's voice was hard.

'And you do that by trying to scare Kate?'

'I knew she wouldn't give up easily. I thought a bit of gentle persuasion would speed things up.'

'Why do you need money so desperately?'

'Gambling debts.'

'How much?'

'None of your business, but over a hundred thousand. They're getting impatient and the only way I could think of getting money fast was by selling the shop. The bank won't advance me any more on my house.'

There was a short pause.

'I'll give you a hundred and fifty thousand for the place,' Ryan snapped at him. 'You can have the money tomorrow.'

'It's worth more than that, and you know it,' Hardwick uttered, still with

Ryan's knee in the small of his back. 'I could get double the amount from the right buyer.'

Ryan shrugged.

'It's up to you. Even if I let you go, and we didn't go to the police, you still haven't dislodged Kate, and she's less likely to move now than she was before. It will take months to find a new buyer. Or have you someone else in mind?'

'I thought the graffiti would do the job, then I tried the pebbles, and after that I thought the telephone calls might do the job, but it didn't work. Sir Lancelot came on his white steed to save her.'

Kate couldn't help herself.

'You were behind the graffiti, too? You're utterly despicable.'

Ryan prodded him further.

'What are you going to do? Either you accept my deal, or we'll call the police and let them sort it out. Perhaps your friends will be waiting for you when you leave the police station.'

'All right, all right. You win.'

'Right. Meet me tomorrow at Dawson's

the solicitors with the deeds. I'll phone them and get an afternoon appointment. Give me your number and I'll let you know what time. When you've signed over the deeds to Kate, I'll give you the money in cash.

'I suggest you never show your face around here again after that. No tricks! I'll be around to make sure you don't make any more trouble.'

'All right! All right! Let me go! You're hurting my arm.'

Ryan waved his mobile phone in Hardwick's face as he got up.

'If you change your mind, or try something funny in future, just remember your admittance to the way you tried to frighten Kate out of the café is here. I have it recorded. If you back out, this is our guarantee for the police.'

Looking angry and very dishevelled, Hardwick struggled to his feet. He scrabbled in his pockets for some paper and a pen, scribbled a number quickly and thrust the note at Ryan. Giving them a parting outraged look, he drifted off down the esplanade muttering to himself.

Ryan threw his arm around Kate.

'He's right,' he remarked. 'The café is worth more. I thought about buying it from him when I realised you meant more to me than I could ever believe. I didn't like him being in charge of your fate.

'I had it valued and made an anonymous offer, but he didn't want to sell at the time. It's a fair price. He'd let it run to ruin. The money will leave him with enough to go on gambling for a while, until he is completely ruined.'

'I'll repay you,' Kate told him. 'I owned my flat and the money from that will be mine any day now. If there isn't enough to cover everything I'll pay you the rest as soon as I can.'

He kissed her.

'Don't worry about it. If things go as I hope they will for us, very soon what's mine will be yours and what's yours will be mine.'

He grinned and held out his arm.

'Shall we go back to your flat and watch the dawn arriving together for the first time? I think, and hope, it will be the first of many we'll share together.'

She tucked her arm through his and decided it felt right.

He tilted his head to the side.

'Can you find a way to have a day off next weekend? We could go for a whole day's sailing.'

'Ryan, please promise me that you don't intend to drag me away from my café all the time to go sailing! I have a café to run, you know.'

'I promise, but even you need days off now and then, and once the café is established you'll be able to afford to employ someone whenever you want a day off, won't you?

'I have the feeling you'll be a good sailor and it would be great if you learned to love sailing as much as I do . . . although that doesn't mean you've got to come with me, of course.'

Kate chuckled. From his attitude and actions, she already knew he would be demanding sometimes, but did she want him to be any different? She didn't, because he declared that he loved her and he never lied.

She knew enough about him to realise Ryan was a caring, intelligent man, someone she could rely on, and someone she could trust and love for the rest of her life.

She vowed she would be his safe harbour, no matter what the future might bring.

Books by Wendy Kremer
in the Linford Romance Library:

REAP THE WHIRLWIND
AT THE END OF THE RAINBOW
WHERE THE BLUEBELLS GROW WILD
WHEN WORDS GET IN THE WAY
COTTAGE IN THE COUNTRY
WAITING FOR A STAR TO FALL
SWINGS AND ROUNDABOUTS
KNAVE OF DIAMONDS
SPADES AND HEARTS
TAKING STEPS
I'LL BE WAITING
HEARTS AND CRAFTS
THE HEART SHALL CHOOSE
THE HOUSE OF RODRIGUEZ
WILD FRANGIPANI
TRUE COLOURS
A SUMMER IN TUSCANY
LOST AND FOUND
TOO GOOD TO BE TRUE
UNEASY ALLIANCE
IN PERFECT HARMONY
THE INHERITANCE
DISCOVERING LOVE

IT'S NEVER TOO LATE
THE MOST WONDERFUL TIME OF THE YEAR
THE SILVER LINING
THE POTTERY PROJECT

Other titles in the Linford Romance Library:

FAR FROM HOME

Jean Robinson

At 23, Dani has an exciting chance at a new life when her mother Francine invites her to live with her in Paris and join her fashion business. What's more, Dani has fallen in love with Claude, Francine's right-hand man. But it's anything but plain sailing at home in England, where Dani has been living with her father, who is on the edge of a breakdown from stress and doesn't want her to leave. What will Dani choose to do — and is Claude willing to wait while she decides?

LEAVING LISA

Angela Britnell

At age seventeen, married with a three-month-old baby and suffering from post-natal depression, all Rosie could see was her life in a cage with a giant lock. Twenty-five years later, after having left her husband Jack and daughter Lisa, she runs her own business in Nashville. But while she's in England, she sees an engagement announcement in the newspaper — Lisa is getting married. And Rosie decides she wants to make contact after all these years, despite fearing their reaction. Will they find room in their hearts for her again?

RUNNING FROM DANGER

Sarah Purdue

Pregnant and alone, Rebecca flees to the US in a bid to escape her ex and his ties to organised crime. There she meets Sheriff Will Hayes in a small backwater town — but can she trust him? When she tries to make a run for it, Will stops her and suggests a plan that involves them both. But Rebecca is unsure of his feelings for her. Can Will keep her safe from her ex and his crime-boss father? Or will the biggest risk come from falling in love?